forbidden WAYS

A romantic companion novel to
Serenity's Plain Secrets

Karen Ann Hopkins

ISBN: 978-1-077-04169-1 (paperback)
ISBN: 978-0-578-53746-7 (ebook)

Books by Karen Ann Hopkins

Serenity's Plain Secrets
in reading order
LAMB TO THE SLAUGHTER
WHISPERS FROM THE DEAD
SECRETS IN THE GRAVE
HIDDEN IN PLAIN SIGHT
PAPER ROSES
EVIL IN MY TOWN
FORBIDDEN WAYS (a romantic companion novel)

Wings of War
in reading order
EMBERS
GAIA
TEMPEST
ETERNITY

The Temptation Novels
in reading order
TEMPTATION
BELONGING
FOREVER
DECEPTION

This one is for my daughters, Lily & Cora. You're my very best friends, and I hope all your dreams come true. Love you both!

ACKNOWLEDGEMENTS

Many thanks to Grace Bell Morris for her continued editing partnership, and to Heather Miller for her proofreading skills. Melissa Stevens and The Illustrated Author created this lovely cover, and the team at EbookPbook provided the interior formatting. I appreciate them all!

And for my loyal readers, who without you and your faithful love and dedication, this book and many others would not be possible. Thank you!!

1

CJ

September 19th
Blood Rock Amish Settlement, Indiana

I stood at the window, watching my sister head down the driveway and turning onto the road. When the car disappeared from sight, I dropped the curtain and jogged into the bathroom. Switching the light on, I swallowed the lump in my throat. I stared at my reflection in the mirror, turning my face to the left and to the right.

The bruising was almost gone. There was just a slight yellowish hue to my one cheek, and the darkness below my eyes resembled dark circles from lack of sleep. The puffiness had disappeared a few weeks ago, and the scratches along my jawline had healed nicely. With a little bit of makeup, no one would know that I'd been nearly beaten to death some eight weeks earlier.

I closed my eyes and stood very still, allowing the memories to flood in.

I was back in the dimly lit little shed. Caleb Johnson was talking. *He had already killed three Amish girls. He had tortured, raped, and murdered them. I knew I was about to die, and that's why I'd inched my way closer to the wall. My heart pounded into my ribcage as I grabbed the hooked cord from the wall. I turned around and struck out with my weapon. The hook hit his cheek with a snap, and he'd reached for his face with a shriek.*

I wrapped my arms around my body and hugged myself. My stomach clenched and my head was thick and heavy. The bathroom disappeared, and I was back in that shed once again.

The adrenaline got my legs pumping without thought. My fingers brushed the doorknob as Caleb's arms closed around my chest. We fell to the floor with a hard jolt to my shoulder.

I kicked up, making contact with his stomach, but it wasn't enough. His fist slammed into my face, knocking me sideways. I drew into a fetal position as he pummeled my head and arms with slaps and punches. Each time he struck me, I flinched but I didn't feel any pain. My mind reeled that he'd gotten me onto the floor, and now he was going to rape and kill me.

He jumped up and grabbed my hair, dragging me to the center of the room. I screamed, feeling sharp pain for the first time. I fought and flailed as I tried to get up, but he kicked me, aiming for my back and legs. One strike hit my face and blood spurted from my nose. The stickiness ran into my mouth, and I gagged on the taste of my own blood.

My limbs became jelly, and each swing I took missed its mark. Caleb rolled me over as he bound me, the thin rope cut into my wrists. He jumped up and stood over me, smiling broadly.

Tears ran down my cheeks and blood continued to trickle from my nose. I shifted, trying to sit up, but the throbbing pain in my back kept me from doing this simple task. I fell backward, my chest heaving and my vision cloudy.

Caleb chuckled low and long. "And you thought you had a chance... really thought you could outsmart me—outmaneuver me. You dumb bitch!" he shouted. "I'm too good for you!"

His last words swirled around in my head. Was he gloating that he'd won, or was he trying to convince his demented mind that he was too good for me? I feared the latter was true, and it had especially been true with the first girl he'd been sweet on. I absently thought of how smart she'd been for pushing him away. As my head swelled, thinking became harder.

"Now I'm going to show you how superior I really am." Caleb's figure was blurry. His hands went to his pants. Next I heard the rattle of a belt and the sound of a zipper.

I couldn't hold it in any longer. I began to scream.

I sucked in a wet gurgling breath and slumped forward, bracing my hands on the sink. I gripped the porcelain tightly and tapped my foot. Taking small breaths, I slowly regained my composure. I was getting better at it. The first time I'd dreamed about the kidnapping and attack, I'd woken soaked in sweat, tearing at the sheets and screaming at the top of my lungs. My sister had held me for several minutes before I had been able to breathe normally again. *Caleb Johnson is dead*, I had to keep telling myself. There was nothing to fear anymore. My friend and the sheriff of Blood Rock, Serenity Adams, had arrived in time to save me and put a bullet in my attacker's head.

I raised my gaze to the mirror. My brown curls had grown longer and my blue eyes were no longer bloodshot. Now that the bruising was nearly gone, I could see the light sprinkling of freckles across my nose. I didn't look half bad, I admitted. I forced thoughts of my captivity to the very back of my mind and exhaled. It was a special day. My sister had just gone back to Indianapolis for good. She'd been here for me during my recovery when I needed her most. She'd played the dutiful sister, and I was thankful for her. But I'd be lying if I said it had been easy. My relationship with my older sister had always been strained. As the days added up after my release from the hospital, those petty childhood dynamics came back into play. The tension had overflowed that very morning when I'd used the last of the coffee creamer she'd bought. She was an expert of making mountains out of mole hills, and I was sure she was as sick of me as I was of her. The creamer was just an excuse to leave. It was unfortunate that we'd had an argument, but the outcome was satisfactory. Eventually she'd call me or I'd text message her. It was inevitable that we'd reconcile once we had some distance between us again. We did love each other after all.

Being alone was freeing. I was glad to get the little cottage back to myself.

I left the bathroom and crawled onto the bed, reaching for the nearest pillow. I drew it against my chest and hugged it. The house was quiet, except for the tick-tock of the mantle clock in the living room. It had belonged to my grandpa. The tapping sound coming from the other room slowed my heart rate and soothed my breathing. My tank top clung to my breasts and little beads of sweat pooled between my cleavage. There wasn't any air conditioning in the cottage, and it was an unusually warm autumn afternoon. I guessed I was lucky, though—at least I had electricity. My landlord and his family did not. They were Amish and lived in the large white house on the hill.

I lifted my head and caught a small breeze from the open window. It carried with it the floral scent of the rose bushes below the windowsill. I inhaled deeply and fell back onto the pillows. A cow mooed in the distance and the faint sound of *clip-clops* on pavement reached my ears. I moaned and buried my face, squeezing my eyes tightly shut.

Maybe I hadn't been fair to my sister. The main reason her presence had annoyed me so deeply was that Joshua Miller had avoided me like the plague after she'd arrived. In the weeks since I'd been home from the hospital, he hadn't visited me once. Even his adorable little daughters had only waved at me as they'd hurried by on their bikes or from their father's buggy. Nana, Joshua's grandmother, had brought food down from the big house every day for nearly two weeks straight, but as time went by, she began to act distant. She tried to make light conversation and she'd gingerly touched my cheek and mumbled something in the Pennsylvania Dutch-German dialect that I didn't understand. Her eyes were full of sorrow, but she never brought up what had happened to me. I figured that the Amish family was having difficulties wrapping their minds around it, but it might have been something else. The bishop of the community, Aaron Esch, had given me a short reprieve to stay in the cottage after the attack. Supposedly he'd felt sorry for me, but I understood my situation here wasn't permanent. Along with healing from the multitude of injuries I'd sustained from Caleb Johnson, I had also been worrying about my future living arrangements.

I thought back to the day I'd moved into the cottage. It had been less than three months ago, but it seemed like much longer. I'd been enchanted by the little house when I'd first stepped foot out of my car. The four-board white fencing, red barns, and rolling green hills had swelled my heart with immediate happiness. It was just what my soul needed after a harsh breakup with an ex-boyfriend who had been cheating on me. In kind of a rush, I'd decided to quit my secretarial job at the precinct in Indianapolis and move out to the country. I was an introvert at heart and I wanted to wallow in my self-pity far from probing eyes. I also wished to return to the passion of my life—painting. What better way to get my creative juices flowing than by moving to an Amish settlement, far away from all my problems in the bustling city? The advertisement in the paper, looking for a renter for the cottage in the countryside, had been just the escape I'd been praying for.

Unfortunately, I wasn't what the landlord had in mind. There had been a misunderstanding with my name—CJ. Joshua Miller thought I was a man, and that's why he'd rented to me. When he'd discovered I was a woman in our first face-to-face meeting, he'd been completely dismayed.

I smiled into the pillow when I recalled how his face had dropped into agitated shock when I'd told him who I was.

The growing sound of hoof beats made me sit up. I swung my legs over the side of the bed and sprinted over to the window. Like a silly goose, I ducked to the side to hide, and peeked out the screen. The breath caught in my throat when I spotted Joshua. He rode a tall black horse, and he was tugging a long rope that was attached to the halter of a smaller gray.

My heart fluttered wildly when he pulled up in front of the cottage and dismounted. He looped the reins over the hitching rail, which was a common structure beside every Amish porch, and then he tied the second horse up. My mouth went painfully dry when he took the porch steps two at a time. The thud of his boots on the wooden boards was immediately followed by rapping on the door.

"Oh, my God. He's actually here," I muttered.

I ran back into the bathroom. I took some tissue paper and quickly dabbed away the sweat between my breasts. I applied some more deodorant and took a swig of mouth wash. I gargled and spit it out. After a quick spritz of body spray, I crunched my curls with my fingers and stepped back. The confidence I'd felt moments before when I'd gazed at my reflection was gone. Now I saw every imperfection, line, and discoloration on my face.

The knocking grew louder.

"Dammit, no time," I hissed.

I shook my head lightly and headed for the front door. It was ridiculous for me to behave like a swoony schoolgirl because Joshua had finally decided to pay attention to me. He was probably just stopping by to collect the rent.

My hand gripped the doorknob, and I closed my eyes and willed my heart to slow down. "It's no biggie, CJ. He's just a widowed Amish guy that's completely unavailable," I mumbled to myself.

I opened the door and my eyes at the same time. A polite smile was frozen on my face when I looked up.

Joshua's hands were on his slim hips and his feet were slightly spread apart. Suspenders stretched from his homespun denim-colored pants, up and over his broad shoulders. His blue shirt sleeves were rolled up to his elbows, exposing tan, toned arms.

He pushed his hat back and his forehead glistened with sweat. His smoky blue eyes widened when he stared back at me.

The warm air in between us was tight with tension and silence.

After the seconds ticked uncomfortably by, Joshua finally found his voice. "It seems like a very long time since we last saw each other," he said roughly.

"It's been about eight weeks. I was in the hospital, and you told me the bishop had said I could stay a while longer. That was the last time you spoke to me."

My cheeks burned and my pulse quickened. Any fool could see I was upset.

He licked his lips and then nodded. His gazed traveled down to my feet and back up to my face. He ignored my statement and my foul mood. "You look good." His voice quieted. "How are you feeling?"

I blew out an irritated sigh and searched his eyes. They darkened a shade. He might really give a damn, but he wasn't going to act like it.

Since he was being conversational, I worked hard to keep it going.

"Pretty much back to normal. My leg still hurts from time to time"—I shrugged—"but not bad. My sister left a little while ago. She's heading back to Indy."

His lips spread into a thin line and he gave a curt nod. "She passed by me on the way out. Will she be back?"

I couldn't stop my mouth from rising into a small smile. "Nope. I think she had enough of me for a while."

He smiled back. The corners of his eyes crinkled. His suntanned face relaxed, almost with a look of relief. "That's good to hear." His smile suddenly disappeared. "I mean, if that's what you want."

I snorted softly. "On a good day, she's annoying. So yeah, I'm happy about it. But it was nice to have someone here when I got out of the hospital to help me recover. I was in pretty bad shape back then. Serenity was so busy wrapping up the investigation, she could only make it out a few times a week." I stared past Joshua's shoulder at the gray horse that stood patiently, swatting flies with its tail. "She probably would have come around more if my sister hadn't been here. They didn't really hit it off very well."

He glanced away, then back again. "I'm sorry I didn't come check in on you. It might not be a sound excuse, but I thought your sister was taking care of you, and you didn't need me around." He let go of a deep breath. "Our friendship also came under the scrutiny of the bishop and the other ministers after you were attacked. I guess word got back to them that I acted overly anxious about your well-being."

My cheeks were on fire. "Friendship?" My eyes narrowed. "Is that what this is—friendship?"

He grunted and drew back. I felt nauseous when he looked back at me. His expression was guarded.

His voice lowered to just above a whisper. "We made a mistake, CJ. I realize that now. You're an Englisher, and that's not going to change. I'm an Amish man, with three children and an elderly grandmother in my household, and that's not going to change." His face twisted, looking pained. "I care deeply for you, but we can't go any further. It would destroy us both in the end."

I struggled for a breath through pinched lips. I couldn't say if it was humiliation that made me feel like my insides were being shredded, or if I really did have feelings for the handsome man who was gazing sternly at me.

In that instant I convinced myself it was my pride. Being dumped by Ryan after two years of dating for a sour-faced coworker had really done a number on my confidence. Now an Amish guy was rejecting me after some flirtatious behavior and a couple of misguided trysts. I was stupid, stupid, stupid.

I spun around and reached for the door. "Okay. I'll start packing." Joshua's hand shot out and grabbed my arm. The firm pressure of his fingers touching my skin jolted my senses. I wondered if he'd felt it too when I slowly turned to face him.

"You don't have to go anywhere. The elders voted on it last night, and it was unanimous. You can continue renting the cottage from me, as long as nothing goes on between us." My mouth fell open in shock, and he quickly added, "It might be because you're close friends with the sheriff, and our community owes Serenity a lot. Or maybe they just decided that it was wrong to force you out because you're a woman." My blood boiled with his words. I was about to speak, but he silenced me with a raised hand. "It doesn't really matter why they changed their minds—as long as they did. You don't have leave, CJ. You can stay as long as you want."

A glint of pleading shined in his eyes and I didn't understand why. Staying in his rental home, acting like we were never lovers, would be torturous. Why would I put myself through that? A little voice in my mind whispered to me—*So you can stay on this beautiful farm and create masterpieces. So you don't have to leave his precious children or his grandmother, who you've grown fond of. So you can be close to Serenity. So you don't have to return, defeated and heartbroken, to Indianapolis.*

Was I strong enough to remain here with the ruggedly handsome Mr. Miller so close by, but completely out of reach? Were all those other things worth the pain of that?

"What do you say?" Joshua coaxed.

His voice deceived him. It had softened to a pitch that told me

9

that the man still had some feelings for me—that he didn't want me to go.

The panic I'd just experienced vanished. I had no idea what game my Amish landlord was playing, but I was determined to win it. I was tired of being manipulated by men. The only way I'd truly be able to move on from my past relationships and become fully independent, was if I faced my demons—and at the moment, Joshua was one of them.

I wondered how he'd feel if I treated him like a platonic friend. Somehow, I knew he wouldn't like it one bit.

"All right, Joshua. I'll stick around for a little while longer."

A smile crept onto his lips, and the look made my belly do a flip.

Had I just made a huge mistake?

"Perfect." His smile turned sly. "How would you like to go for a horseback ride?"

I felt my eyes bulge and my head began to spin. The Amish man really was insane, I decided.

2

JOSHUA

The shocked look on CJ's face was worth the risk of inviting her horseback riding. The idea had formed in my mind and flew straight out of my mouth in the blink of an eye. It was foolish, I admit, but I couldn't take back the offer.

She stared at me with wide, green eyes that reminded me of early springtime grass. I tried not to notice her full, pouty lips, but failed. A ball developed in my throat and I swallowed it down. So much for staying away from CJ West.

"Are you serious?" Her voice rose higher. "You just informed me that we made a mistake, and now you're talking about horseback riding? Are you ten years old?"

Her face flushed and her brows curved into an angry scowl. I chuckled at her fierce look and her head snapped sideways. I threw my hand up to fend off her possible outburst. "I just bought this mare from Samuel Yoder." I gestured to the gray horse. "She's a sweetheart. I thought that after weeks of convalescing, you might enjoy some fresh air and exercise. Do you know how to ride?"

Her gaze flicked from the horse back to me. "Of course, I can ride a horse." Her concerned expression wasn't convincing me though. She looked around. "Where is your family?"

"They're spending the day at Joseph and Katherine Bender's. There's a barn raising over there, and the children are helping with the food and drinks. I'm signed up to help tomorrow. Nana is assisting with Laura Coblenz's birthing." He shrugged a little. "I have a free day."

"Won't you get into trouble?"

I appreciated the strained sound of her voice. Even after what I said to her, she still worried about my reputation in the community.

I balled my fists. "No one will know. We can hack through the trails behind the farm, away from prying eyes."

"Why?"

It was one simple word, but I had no good answer for it. My invitation was wrong on every level. I strained to say something sensible.

"CJ, you've been through so much. I feel regret that I haven't been there for you…since you…were taken by that man." I struggled for the right words to say. "Even though a romantic relationship between us is forbidden, I still want to be your friend."

CJ's eyes filled with understanding and remorse. It was the look of longing she cast toward the gray mare that made me hopeful.

"Well, it's been a while since I was on the back of a horse."

"How long is a while," I asked carefully.

She stared off into space. "I guess I was about fifteen. My neighbor had a couple of horses and we'd go out riding together. There was a summer that we rode almost every single day." She eyed me. "This one time we were alongside the road, and a car full of guys drove by, honking at us. My horse jumped sideways and lost her footing. She stumbled, and I went right over her shoulder. My head hit the pavement pretty hard. When I came to, my friend said I was out for about thirty seconds."

"Was that the last time you rode?"

She shook her head. "No, but I wasn't as anxious to climb on board as I was before the accident. The horse—her name was Gypsy—was fine and all, and it was just because of the rude behavior of some stupid kids, but the ordeal still scared me. Before that incident, I'd never even thought about falling off."

I nodded encouragingly. "I promise we won't be near a road, and Samuel's little girls have been riding this mare all summer long. You'll be safe."

CJ was a petite little thing, but at my words she straightened up taller. "I'm not afraid." She jogged down the steps, up to the horse. "What's her name?"

I shifted my hat and scratched my head. "I reckon I don't know what the Yoders were calling her." I stepped off the porch. "She's a fine-looking mare, though. She needs just the right name."

CJ glanced over her shoulder. She was caressing the horse's face tenderly. I watched her hands work against the hair and a shudder passed through me. "Do you have any ideas?" she asked.

Her voice was excited, and I was suddenly grateful for inviting her. Sure, I was taking a chance. If anyone saw us riding alone together, I'd be in big heap of trouble with the elders—the entire community for that matter. But at that moment, seeing CJ's beaming face, nothing else mattered. In the sunlight, the soft hues of bruising on her cheek were barely visible. Still, when I noticed the mark, my muscles tightened. I hadn't been there to help her when that lunatic took her captive. The least I could do was to create an opportunity to make her smile. Even if it meant life would be terribly dangerous for me. It wasn't just about if anyone in the community found out that I was still spending time with my beautiful tenant. CJ posed a very different kind of risk—one that involved my heart.

"I hadn't really thought about it. What do you want to call her?"

Her eyes widened. "You'd let me name her?"

"Of course." I grinned. "Well, unless you come up with something silly or inappropriate, that is."

She laughed and I enjoyed the sound.

"She looks just like my friend's horse I used to ride, and I always loved the name Gypsy. What do you think?"

"Gypsy it is," I replied, untying the horse. I handed the lead rope to CJ and fetched my own horse.

"We're going to ride right now?" The words nearly jumped from her mouth.

"Sure. It'll be dark in a few hours. We don't want to waste the time we've been given."

"Right." She tugged on the rope and headed toward the stable.

I followed her, glancing at the roadway. The coast was clear, and when I strained to listen, I didn't hear any buggy travel. I was glad CJ moved with long strides, and I blew out a breath of relief when she disappeared into the barn.

CJ took the job of grooming the new horse very seriously. I found myself waiting beside her, holding the saddle in my arms, and pushing dirt around with the toe of my boot. She ran the brush over the horse with a light, slow touch. Gypsy's eyes were closed. I feared the mare was falling asleep.

"Are you stalling, or are you really that deliberate when brushing a horse?"

She put the brush into the caddy and turned around. "It's nice to groom a horse. I used to enjoy the grooming the most—even more than the riding part."

Her white shirt was smudged with dirt and it clung snugly to her chest, allowing me to view her pale skin and the dip in between her breasts. The rise and fall of her breathing accentuated her shapely figure. My pulse quickened, and I moved past her, depositing the saddle pad onto Gypsy's back first, and then lowering the western saddle down on top of it.

"You're welcome to groom my horses anytime." I tried to keep my voice nonchalant. I would not do anything to invite this woman's attention on me. Because the Lord knew, I wouldn't be strong enough to say no to her.

"Really—are you serious?" Her voice quaked with enthusiasm.

"It would be a great help to John. My son's in charge of the horse care, and with us harvesting the tomatoes and corn, he's slacked off a bit lately.

"You can count on me. I'll make sure they all look their best."

When I glanced over, CJ was touching my horse's neck, looking very serious.

"If I had realized you liked horses so much, I would have put you to work sooner," I teased.

She took the reins and followed me down the barn aisle to the back doorway. She was quiet and I was trying to think up something to say when she spoke first.

"I wasn't up to it until this week. My entire body ached, but my ribs were the worst. I could hardly catch a breath for the pain in my chest."

A rusty breath scraped my throat and I tried not to envision that monster kicking and hitting CJ, over and over again.

If I dwelled on the horrifying image, an anger so hot and vile gripped my heart that I felt like I might lose my mind.

I couldn't stop my hand from brushing her arm when she stopped alongside me. She jerked away from my touch and placed her foot in the stirrup.

"Do you require assistance?" I stepped behind her to lift her up.

"No, I've got this," she insisted. She winced and sucked in a sharp breath as she hoisted herself up.

15

My hands hovered beneath her, ready to catch her or even shove her the rest of the way to avoid her straining herself further. When I had impulsively asked her to join me on a joyride, I hadn't been thinking about her battered ribs.

Her leg was stiff, but she managed to swing it over the horse's back. She straightened in the saddle and smirked down at me. "See. I got on by myself."

I hid my smile as I turned to my horse and swung into the saddle. "Yes, you did. You're an amazing woman, CJ West."

She raised her chin and the side of her mouth lifted higher. "Yeah, too bad I'm not Amish."

3

CJ

My heels bumped Gypsy's sides and I squeezed with my thighs when she sped up into a trot, leaving Joshua and his wolfish grin, behind. I had looked away before I said the *too bad I'm not Amish* thing. I don't know what had come over me. The words fell out of my mouth before I could stop them. Now my face burned with embarrassment and guilt. Joshua was trying to be nice. Just because he wasn't in a position to explore a relationship with me wasn't his fault. It was just the way it was. There was no need for me to be snide about it.

The bouncing sent jolts of pain through my ribcage, and I pulled back on the reins, bringing Gypsy back down to a lumbering walk. I carefully took shallow breaths, but it still hurt like hell. I looked straight ahead when the pounding hooves caught up.

"Whoa, there. You might be overdoing it a bit, don't you think?"

I rolled my eyes. Joshua obviously didn't understand that I took off just to get away from him. Now our knees were practically brushing each other as he stared at me with tight concern on his usually cautious face.

I forced out a little laugh, trying not to sound pained. "I'm fine." I glanced over. "Perhaps staying at a walk for the time being is advisable." I settled into the deep seat and couldn't helping sighing contentedly. Tall grass that nearly reached the bottom of my tennis shoes swayed in the warm breeze. The sun was beginning to lower in the western sky, but it still shone brightly down on our heads. We skirted a small pond and dozens of dragon flies zipped around above the rippling water. "It sure is nice to be back in the saddle," I said quietly, almost to myself. "You notice things on the back of a horse that you wouldn't normally." I pointed at the opposite slope, where a fox darted over the knoll. "Look!"

"I hope it doesn't go after my chickens or I'll have to take care of it," Joshua said gruffly.

My head snapped in his direction. He was shading his eyes with his hand and searching where the orange animal had gone.

"You had better not hurt it," I growled

When he turned, his face was scrunched. "Foxes kill and eat chickens. My children and Nana eat eggs from our flock each and every day. If a fox or other predator becomes a problem, it could mean less food on my family's table—and a bunch of dead chickens." His look was steady. "Is that what you want?"

A bird cackled on a nearby tree branch and my gaze followed the sound. It flew to a closer tree and I craned my neck to get a better look at it as I exhaled a deep breath. Joshua's sensible recitation about the problem of having a fox on the farm sunk in, and it annoyed me.

His horse moved closer still. If I wanted to, I could have easily leaned over and given the man a kiss. My eyes strayed to him. He sat straight in his saddle, looking like he'd been born there. His hands were relaxed on the reins and he swayed with the movements of the black animal. And he was watching me, too.

I was the first to look away. "Do you always have to be so practical?" I asked.

"Why wouldn't I be?"

I smiled to myself. It was kind of a stupid question to ask an Amish man. "Couldn't you just enjoy seeing a beautiful wild animal? Your first thought was about killing it," I scolded.

Joshua's eyes widened and his mouth opened with a quick retort, but he paused. His jaw snapped shut and he shook his head. He slumped a little and when he spoke, his voice was mellow. "I did notice the animal's beauty." He shrugged a little. "Foxes fascinated me as a child. I used to watch the kits playing in the field behind our house." He glanced back and his expression was somber. "It was my little secret. I didn't tell my brothers or my parents how close the fox family was to our home. One day, I was hoeing the garden for Ma, and I heard a commotion in the hen house. I ran to the building as fast as my legs would carry me. When I arrived, I discovered a fox had dug into the enclosure at the corner and had a buff hen clamped between its jaws. Two other chickens were already dead on the ground." He shook his head. "At first, I just stood there, stunned, but then the poor hen began squawking shrilly and my limbs began to move again. As that fox tried to squeeze back under the wire, I hit it with the tool that was still in my hands. I killed the animal, and miraculously, the hen that it had in its mouth survived the ordeal. When Pa came home, he went out in the back field with my oldest brother. I had hidden in the barn loft when they had left, so I wouldn't have to go with them. I heard six gun shots fired that evening. I never asked about it afterwards. I guess I didn't really want to know what had happened to the baby foxes who jumped and yapped at each other like puppies."

"That's awful," I breathed. I shook the image from my mind and focused on twirling Gypsy's mane between my fingertips.

"Do you hate me for killing the fox?" Joshua asked plainly.

"Of course not. You had to save your chicken. I understand that, and you were only a kid."

"If I had chased the fox family away from the farm when I'd first spotted them, they might not have been tempted to begin nabbing the chickens. I was foolish and selfish—and those pretty animals paid the price."

I risked a sideways glance. Joshua was staring off into the distance, lost in his own thoughts. Even though a part of me was still miffed that he'd flirted enough with me that I actually had started to seriously like him, I still hated to see him so distracted about a bad childhood memory. He wouldn't even have thought about it if I hadn't been so harsh.

"It's probably best if we discourage any foxes from living here so close to your farm," I conceded. "That doesn't mean you have to immediately shoot the poor creature. It might even have babies of its own to feed."

Joshua looked straight ahead. "Yes, perhaps it does."

I was tired of talking about foxes. The path led into a stand of trees. It was just barely wide enough for two horses abreast, but Joshua didn't stray from my side. Our legs rubbed as we entered the cooler shade under the branches. I inhaled the tangy scent of pine needles. Shadows stretched beneath the limbs, and the birds were silent. The woods had a magical feeling that made me imagine fairies and unicorns. The only sound was the squeaking of our leather saddles as we swayed back and forth.

My eyes fluttered and I felt drowsy. It was a wonderful sensation that I hadn't experienced in a long time. Anxiety had plagued me after the attack. Every time I had closed my eyes, I'd seen Caleb's twisted face looking back at me. The counseling sessions had helped a little, but not enough. This ride had done more for my mental health than a month of therapy had accomplished.

The silence became deafening and I realized that I really did want to talk to Joshua. "What's your horse's name?" I blurted out. My voice sounded loud and unwelcome and I closed my eyes, wishing I'd remained silent.

He leaned down and patted the black neck. "Desperado."

I laughed and Joshua's brows arched. I had to suck in my mirth to speak. "That's quite the name for an Amish horse."

"I didn't name him, of course. He came with it." He tilted his head and looked sideways at me. "I could have called him something different, maybe a biblical name, like Abraham. Would that be what you expected?"

His voice was playful, and I enjoyed the sound of it. "Maybe, but Desperado is the perfect name for him." My gaze traveled over the tall black horse, with a mane that was so long and thick, it draped over both sides of his neck. "He's gorgeous."

Pride glinted in Joshua's blue eyes when they met mine. "You're a real horsewoman, CJ. I never would have guessed it."

"A wannabe, for sure. When I was a kid, I'd read anything with a horse in it. My favorite books were Black Beauty and the Black Stallion." I let out a long, wispy breath. "I always wanted a horse of my own."

"Well, now you have one," Joshua said firmly.

I stared at him. Was he serious?

Every time his leg brushed mine, there was a jolt to my heart. I didn't like the feeling or the melancholy that came with it. Even though there was definitely chemistry between the two of us, and we enjoyed each other's company, nothing could come from it. We were destined for friendship and nothing else.

"That's nice of you, but it won't last long. I'm sure you bought this little mare for your daughters, and it's not like I can take her with me when I leave."

He paused and seemed to gather his words carefully. "Yes, I thought she'd be a good ride for Nora, and then Sylvia could have the pony."

I remembered how mean the little black pony, Ranger, was, and shook my head lightly at the idea of Joshua's six-year-old daughter handling him.

"Even though Gypsy is a full-size horse, I think she's a better fit for Sylvia," I suggested.

A strange look flitted across Joshua's face. It almost looked like regret.

"You like to talk about leaving," he said.

I shrugged and searched the shards of blue sky through the tree branches. A bug buzzed near my ear, but I didn't bother to swat it away. Instead, I pondered why Joshua was giving me mixed messages. He had stated right off the bat that there was no chance of a relationship between us. Yet here he was, bumping legs with me on a private horseback ride through the woods, and offering to give me a horse. Why did he look so bothered that I wasn't staying forever? It made no sense at all.

"I really appreciate that you're being so nice to me, Joshua, but honestly, I think it's better if I start making plans to move out." I took a deep breath that jabbed into my ribs. "It's just too awkward to continue renting from you after what happened between us."

His lips pursed and he nodded agreement. I was hoping he'd say something to give me hope, or that he had changed his mind in the time that we'd saddled up. But he was a smart and practical man. He knew it was best that I left.

"Are you happy with your lifestyle?"

The question startled me. I wasn't sure if it was his arrogant tone or the words themselves. "I don't know what you mean. Nobody's life is perfect, but I'm trying." I pushed my curls back. "My original plan when I moved out here was to get back into art. When I was in college, I sold some paintings, making a decent income. But there were outside forces, like my mom and sister, pushing me to get a *real job*. They never believed I could make a living as an artist. When I look back now, I feel like I sold out on my dream. I had been building a name for myself and networking with galleries and other artists. I could have made it, but I quit, choosing an easier path." I stroked Gypsy's warm fur and gawked at the panoramic view as we stepped out from the cover of the trees into an open field. Purple, yellow, and white flowers dotted the grass, flooding my senses with the perfume of thousands of wildflowers. The hills sloped gently, and the metal roofs of Joshua's house and barns glared brightly in the waning sunlight. Inspiration gripped my heart and I turned back to Joshua. "I have enough savings to get by for a couple more months without having to get a regular job. Now that I'm feeling better, I want to crank out some folksy, rural-inspired artwork for a possible show back in Indianapolis next spring."

With each stride Gypsy took, we were getting closer and closer to home—or at least Joshua's home. I hated that the ride was ending so soon. Joshua had snagged a long piece of grass and it now rested between his lips. He stared ahead, brooding.

When he broke the silence, his voice was level, unreadable. "You're a woman in your early thirties, and your plan for the future doesn't involve marriage or children?"

My head rolled and I barked out a coarse laugh. "That's one of the problems I have with your society—that women are defined by their marriages and how many kids they have."

"That's not true. Many wives are partners in business with their husbands. They do the book keeping and help make important decisions, but there's nothing wrong with having a family, too."

His tone had turned biting and I pressed my lips together.

"Someday I'll probably meet the right person and we'll get married and have a couple of kids together—and that would be very nice, but I'm not going to focus on that happening. I want to finally follow my dream of being an artist. I think a woman can achieve everything she wants if she sets her mind to it."

Joshua chuckled and my head quickly turned his direction. "I trust a woman like you could achieve all those things, but wouldn't it be easier to create paintings if you didn't have to worry about a full-time job?"

"Well, sure, but—" like a sucker punch to my face, I understood what Joshua was insinuating. "You think I should run out and find a husband to support me while I pursue my art career?"

"No, that's not what I meant. I simply was trying to point out that women with husbands can have time to do other things because their needs are being provided for."

"I don't think I'd have a lot of time to paint if I had several toddlers running around." I clenched my teeth.

He paused and then mumbled, "True enough."

I became brave with his agreement. "You asked me if I liked my lifestyle. What about you—do you like being Amish?"

He glanced at me tentatively. "I am content being Amish. Even as a teenager, I had no thoughts about running away to the English world, like so many of our youth. I enjoy farming the land. I appreciate our simplistic lives." He lifted his shoulders. "Our way is more difficult than yours, I admit."

"Like driving cars…" I tried to keep any mocking from my voice.

He mused for a moment. "That is something I do regret sometimes—mostly the convenience, though. We hire drivers to take us places we need to go, and without that particular freedom, we find ourselves spending more time with our families and at our homes. It's a tradeoff I readily accept."

"What about electricity? Don't you miss that? And why can't you have electricity anyway?" I plowed on.

"So many questions all of a sudden." He rubbed his chin. "I'm surprised Serenity didn't explain some of these things to you."

"Oh, she tried, but she's just as confused about half of it as I am."

He nodded slowly. "We don't want electricity because it brings a line of connection into our homes from the outside."

I looked back at him with my brows knitted and thought hard about what he said. He laughed and kicked out playfully with his foot in a moment of lightheartedness. "Some things you'll never understand unless you're one of us, CJ. Don't ponder too much. You'll give yourself a headache."

The house was close enough to make out the small details of the window panes and flower boxes. Martins darted in and out of the white painted gourds hanging in the yard. The maple leaves were drying out, turning bright yellow and reminding me that crisper weather was on the way.

"It's all very strange." I faced him and leaned back in the saddle. "You're right. I'll never be Amish, so I don't have to know everything."

He began to speak, thought better of it, and fell into a moody silence. I squeezed Gypsy into a faster walk, putting a few feet of distance between us.

"Da! Da!" a voice called out urgently in the distance.

Joshua spurred his horse into a gallop and flew past me, heading toward the barnyard. Dust flew up in my face and I coughed, grabbing my side as I bumped Gypsy into a trot.

When I finally made it back to the stable, Joshua was off of his horse, talking to John. The thirteen year old was holding the reins to the bay gelding he usually rode. I realized that I didn't know the name of that particular horse, either.

My ribs were throbbing when I pulled up alongside the man and his son. They were talking excitedly in their language, and at first, I didn't pay a lot of attention to them. I was in some discomfort, and I wasn't even sure I could dismount without assistance. When I heard the words, "Sylvia" and "injured," I perked up.

"What's happened to Sylvia?"

Joshua looked up in surprise, like he'd forgotten all about me. He glanced back at his son and said something. It was then that I noticed the shocked look on the boy's freckled face. Joshua and I weren't supposed to be seen riding alone together. The father would have some explaining to do.

"She was climbing a tree with the other children, and she fell. The women think her arm might be broken." Joshua rushed the words out.

Somehow, without any thought or recollection, I was off the horse and standing beside Joshua. "We have to go to her."

Joshua's face tightened. He ignored me, speaking English to his son. "Unsaddle the horses. I'll hire a driver to take me over to the Yoder's farm."

At that moment I didn't care about secrecy or Amish decorum. "That's ridiculous! I can drive you over there." He turned hard eyes on me and I knew he was going to deny my offer, so I quickly added in a steadier voice. "It would save a lot of time. I'm sure the poor kid is in pain. She needs to see a doctor as quickly as possible."

John looked between his father and me. He took a breath and mumbled something to Joshua. Whatever the kid said, helped. Joshua gestured me to join him as he aimed for my car.

I handed John my reins. He nodded and managed to flash a rigid smile.

I quickly retrieved my car keys from the kitchen table in the cottage and joined Joshua, who was already waiting in the passenger seat.

I started the engine. "Don't worry, I'm sure she'll be fine."

The cab tingled with the electricity of conflict. "I have simply hired you to drive me to retrieve my daughter." His gaze was unyielding. "You must not act familiar with me, CJ. Everyone will be watching."

I pressed the gas down a little too hard turning onto the road, and Joshua, who hadn't bothered with a seatbelt, jerked into the door.

A thank you would have been nice, but no. I got a lecture instead.

I refused to look at the Amish man or respond to what he'd just said. It was moments like these when my resolve hardened.

Joshua Miller wasn't the man for me.

4

JOSHUA

When I walked up, Sylvia was seated at the picnic table, surrounded by a crowd of women and children. I swiftly cleared a path with waving hands so that I could reach my child. Sylvia's face was red and tear-streaked from crying. She cradled her injured arm, and her head bobbed up and down with her gasps.

I knelt in front of her and my youngest child slid into my lap. "Why were you climbing a tree?" I pressed my head to hers and lifted her up.

She stopped crying and hiccupped a sharp breath. "It was Nora that made me do it. At first, she said I wasn't big enough, and when I argued, she told me to go ahead and climb to the top."

I searched the sea of children's faces until I found my oldest daughter. She had just turned ten, and out of all of my children, she reminded me the most of her mother. Her large, brown eyes were sullen and when they met mine, I saw her wince. I nodded my head at CJ's car with a jerk, and without saying a word, Nora marched by the other children with her head held high and her arms crossed. Her dress was just as smudged as Sylvia's was, and she hadn't even fallen out of a tree.

I let out an agitated breath and held Sylvia closer, murmuring, "You'll be fine, baby girl." I carefully probed her limp arm until she squealed out. I drew my fingers back. "Looks like it might be broken."

"Yes, I'd wager it is."

My attention paused on a young woman I had never met before. She stared brazenly back at me. She was tall, just a few inches shy of my height, and slender. Her maroon dress was covered with a wide apron, a style worn back in Lancaster. It was spotted with dirt, and so were her fingers. When my gaze strayed to her cap, I saw it was soiled too.

"Let me guess, you're a gardener, not a doctor?" I said lightly.

Her tan cheeks darkened a shade and her gray eyes sparked. She tucked a stray blonde lock back up under her cap. "Yes, I was in the garden, when Sylvia tumbled from the tree. I put ice on it. I have experience with healing both flowers and people."

Sylvia took a gulp and began crying again. I backed away, anxious to get her into the car. "I don't believe we've met…"

Anna Bachman appeared at my elbow. She pressed a wet cloth to Sylvia's face, wiping away her tears. "This is Rosetta Bontrager. She's going to be staying in our community for a short time."

"Nice to meet you," I said politely. "Thank you for assisting my child."

She folded her hands on her apron and nodded.

"CJ! You came to save me again?" Sylvia's words made my heart rate spike.

I turned to see that CJ had left her car and was standing a few feet away, holding Nora's hand. Sylvia stopped crying and reached out to CJ with her good hand. CJ's face flushed, but she didn't hesitate to come toward my daughter.

I stood still, trying to keep my face neutral.

"I sure did, but I know how tough you are. Falling from a tree is nothing to getting flung off an angry pony," CJ said. She touched Sylvia's cheek and the child smiled.

"That's right," Sylvia sat up taller in my arms, her arm suddenly not as painful. "I am tough. See, Nora. CJ thinks I'm tough."

All eyes were staring at CJ—and me. Rosetta's gaze was especially intent. So much for trying not to draw any attention to CJ West. I made a grunting sound in my own head.

I faced Anna. "It was a blessing that CJ was able to drop her own plans to bring me to my daughter."

Anna's brows rose. "Of course." She touched CJ's shoulder lightly. "Thank you for helping out. Sometimes we are in need of more speed than a buggy can provide."

Katherine Bender stepped up and laughed. "Isn't that the truth!" She winked at CJ. "It's nice to see you again. One of these days, you should stop by for some fresh lemon tea and a visit. It seems whenever I see you there's a calamity of some sort."

CJ broke into a grin. "Sounds good. I would enjoy that."

I didn't know that the women were friends. The news unsettled me some, but looking at CJ's bright face, I let the uncomfortable sensation go. Women needed companionship. The only friend CJ had that I knew of was Sheriff Serenity Adams—and that crass woman's personality was more manlike in a lot of ways.

I placed Sylvia into the backseat next to her sister and slid in after her. The child climbed back into my lap when I was seated, reminding me of when she was a baby and she'd fall asleep in my arms most nights. Her eyelids fluttered, and then drooped closed.

"Da."

"Yes, baby?"

"Am I going to see Mama soon?"

Her words made me catch my breath. CJ's eyes flicked to the rearview mirror and met mine. Sylvia was only five when her mother had drowned. Miranda's buggy had been swept into the river when a bridge gave way during a flood. It had appeared to be a freak accident, but I knew right away something was amiss. My wife was afraid of horses, and would never have been out on the roadway on that fateful day unless she was out of her mind. And in a way, she had been. She'd suffered from depression after the birth of our little boy. When it became too much for her, she suffocated the baby in the crib. When she'd confessed to me what she'd done, I had said some horrible things to her. It was that same day that she harnessed the horse to the buggy and left in the storm. No one knew the truth except for me and CJ. I had told her the story in a weak moment.

A wave of emotions surged through my body. Regret, remorse, and confusion almost overwhelmed me. I squeezed my youngest child tighter. "Why would you say something like that?"

"Because she thinks she's dying," Nora piped up.

"Oh, child. Your arm will mend. I promise," I said.

"But I want to see Mama," she cooed.

I closed my eyes. An image of Miranda appeared in my mind. She had been a beautiful woman on the outside, but beneath the smooth, pale skin, she was a monster. I would never forgive my wife for murdering our son, even if CJ thought I should let it go and forgive. A cool sweat broke out on my brow when I thought about how lucky little Sylvia was that she hadn't died at her own mother's hands as well. It was a secret she'd never know about. As hard as it was, I had no choice but to perpetuate my surviving children's belief that their mother was a good and kind woman.

I swallowed the bitter taste in my mouth and prepared to say something to comfort the child, when I glanced down and saw that she was fast asleep.

The rest of the trip to town was silent. Wind blew in from the cracked windows and Nora rested her head on my arm. I watched as the passing farms changed into suburban houses and businesses.

CJ pulled up to the emergency entrance of Blood Rock's hospital and looked over the seat. "I'll run in and get a nurse."

My chest tightened. I raised my hand. "That won't be necessary. I'll take Sylvia in myself."

Her face paled. "All right, then. I can take Nora to the diner for a bite to eat, so you can focus on Sylvia."

I shook my head and ignored the look of wide anticipation on Nora's face. "Come on, Nora, you're coming with me and your sister." I forced myself to look into CJ's eyes. There was hurt there. "I'm sure we'll be a little while. I can call a driver to pick us up when we're finished here. You shouldn't wait for us."

I left the car with Sylvia still asleep in my arms, and Nora clinging to a wad of my shirt.

I didn't look back. I knew if I did, I would have changed my mind about allowing CJ to come with us.

5

CJ

I took a gulp of sweet tea and stared at my uneaten food. All the optimism I'd felt during the horseback ride had vanished when Joshua went back to treating me like I was a just some random woman who drove him around sometimes. Rubbing the side of my forehead didn't erase the memories of Joshua's penetrating blue gaze, or the way his usually stoic face came alive when he actually smiled. If anything, the gyrations made the man become even more firmly cemented in my mind.

"Sorry I'm late," Serenity said, sliding into the booth. She was in full sheriff uniform, minus the hat. Her blonde hair was pulled back into the usual ponytail, and for a change, the expression on her face was fairly relaxed. "Todd decided to get a stomach bug, and I had to finish up his paperwork for him."

"Poor Todd. I hope he gets over it soon. Digestive issues are the worst." I attempted to take my mind off my own miserable existence.

Serenity laughed and I leaned back. Her grin was wicked when she said, "A few days out of my hair isn't such a bad thing."

"You two have an interesting relationship," I offered.

She shrugged. "He's been annoying me since we were kids. Because of our long-standing friendship, he thinks he can tell me what to do, sometimes forgetting that I'm the sheriff." Her eyes were lively and her expression easy. Her angst about Todd was superficial. It almost seemed like she enjoyed sparring with her partner.

"What's he bugging you about now?"

"The wedding." When my brows rose, she added, "Yep. He thinks Daniel and I should tie the knot this fall, but I'm not ready. There's too much going on. I'm still finishing up the court documents relating to the Amish girl murders." She paused and frowned. "You doing okay?"

I glanced away and back again. Serenity looked thoughtful as she waited patiently for me to answer. "Yeah, sure. Physically, I'm a lot better. Mentally—it's tough."

"Are you still seeing the therapist?"

I nodded. "My sister left today."

Serenity cracked a smile. "Good riddance, I say. She was a bitch."

Between Serenity's words and the *damn-straight* look on her face, I laughed. The jarring movement caused my ribs to hurt again. I sucked in my mirth and smiled back at her. "I agree wholeheartedly, but you never said anything that made me think you felt that way."

She shrugged. "I'm a good actor. You needed her help at the time, so I put up with her rude comments. But honestly, if she hadn't left, the next time she said something about how lame my town was, I was going to let her have it." She waved to Nancy, the owner of the diner, to come over. "I'll have the usual," she ordered.

"Coming right up." Nancy paused, placing her hand on her hip that was thrusted up. For a woman who had to be pushing seventy, she had the manners of a much younger person. Her dyed red hair was piled in a loose bun and her make up accentuated her cobalt eyes, deepening the lines on her face. Her expression was coy. "Serenity, I heard it's going to be an autumn ceremony."

In one quick motion, Serenity wadded up a napkin and tossed it at Nancy. Nancy was quick and caught it in the air. Her cackling laugh drew the attention of several nearby patrons as she turned on her heel and headed back to the counter.

"Does everyone in town need to know my business?" she snarled. The agitated look disappeared from her face when she crossed her arms on the table and leaned forward. "Seriously, are you going to be all right out there by yourself?"

I pressed my lips together and fought off the wave of emotion that threatened to make my eyes tear up. "I suppose so, but I'm not really alone, am I? There's a family right up the driveway that I'm quite fond of."

Serenity's eyes widened and I braced for her words of warning.

"The last time we talked, you said they hadn't really communicated with you at all—especially Joshua."

I met her concerned gaze. "Today the silence was broken. Joshua invited me to go for a horseback ride."

Her mouth dropped, but she quickly recovered. "What did you say?"

"I said yes." My stomach churned under Serenity's scrutiny.

She glanced around, and lowered her voice. "Have you lost your mind? That stupid Amish man is even crazier than I thought." She slumped back and thudded her head on the back of the red plastic cushion. "I worry about you, CJ."

"I know we talked about all this, and I had decided to end whatever was going on between us, but that was before Joshua told me I could stay in the cottage."

Serenity's eyes rounded. "The elders agreed to that?"

"Yep. I guess the bishop felt sorry for me or something."

The waitress deposited Serenity's cola, fries, and hamburger on the table. Serenity ignored the food. "That doesn't make any sense," she said.

The corner of my mouth lifted. "The bishop isn't so bad. Maybe he's letting go of some of his stuffiness and relaxing the rules."

She shook her head. "No. There's a better chance of it snowing here in July than for the bishop and ministers to ease up on their restrictive lifestyle." She popped a french fry into her mouth. "It must be something else."

"Like what?" My pulse quickened. Serenity was cynical most of the time, but she had great instincts about people and their motives. I held my breath.

"The bishop is testing Joshua Miller." She said it in a matter-of-fact way and then bit into her burger.

"That might explain why Joshua went from a super friendly nice guy, to being completely embarrassed to have me standing next to him in front a crowd of his people," I said.

"What's with the crowd?" she asked.

I took another sip from my drink. "His little girl fell out of a tree this afternoon. I think her arm's broken. I offered to drive him over to the farm where most of the community was gathered to raise a barn."

She nodded, taking another bite. I wished I could work up that kind of appetite. "Makes sense he'd act frosty toward you. They're good people on most days, but one thing I learned early on is that they act especially frigid when they're all together. And they're always watching."

I drew in a deep breath and exhaled slowly. "I don't know what to do, Serenity. I love the cottage and living on that beautiful farm. The place inspires me, but now that I'm up and moving around again, I'm afraid that seeing Joshua on a daily basis will drive me crazy."

"It'll hurt like hell," she agreed.

"What should I do?" I searched her face, hoping I didn't sound like a mindless teenager. I had always wrestled with indecision, and that was probably one of the reasons I wasn't where I wanted to be career wise or on a personal level. Serenity didn't have that problem. She made up her mind, for good or bad, and jumped right in. I envied her unwavering personality.

She chewed her food slowly, swallowed, and took a sip of her cola. By the time she opened her mouth, I was terrified of what she would say. "If I were you, I'd stay there just long enough to crank out some of those whimsical country paintings you keep talking about. You aren't going to find a better backdrop than at that farm. You just got a big win with the elders. Hold yourself together and ignore Joshua. He's not worth your time."

"Who's not worth CJ's time?"

Elayne Weaver, the town's assistant DA, and former resident of the Amish community, bumped into Serenity's side, forcing her to move over in the booth. Serenity rolled her eyes and growled a little as she slid over to make room for the tall brunette.

Elayne's eyes flew open with speculation and her lips were pursed and pouty. I still hadn't decided if I liked the gorgeous woman. She seemed to just annoy Serenity, but I sensed a deeper connection between the two women than Serenity led on.

"Are you by chance talking about the dashing Joshua Miller?" Elayne asked in low purr.

"Shh!" Serenity hissed, looking around. When she had stopped searching for spies, she glared at Elayne. "Show a little stealth, would you. Of all people, you should know how to do that."

Elayne frowned, but she nodded after a long pause. When she looked across the table, she was back to her perky self. She whispered, "Sorry, I was excited. I just heard the news that you're not being kicked off the Miller property."

Serenity turned to Elayne. "How do you get information so quickly?"

She lifted her shoulders and grinned. "I have my ways, that's all."

"I haven't decided whether I'm staying," I said quietly. Serenity rolled her eyes and I avoided her frown.

Elayne placed a warm hand over mine and I resisted the urge to pull it away. "You've had a rough time of it, we all know that—but you survived. Why give up now?"

"Give up on what?" I glanced between the two women. Elayne's smile deepened, like she knew my darkest secrets. Serenity's eyes shot up again. Her arm was propped on the table and she rested her head on her palm, looking bored.

"I know you're sweet on Joshua, and I bet he feels the same way about you," Elayne said.

"Why does it matter?" Serenity came alive, swiveling like a snake about to strike. She lowered her voice. "He's Amish, She's not. It's impossible. So why should she get all frustrated and have her heart broken?" Serenity admonished.

Elayne winced but kept looking straight at me. "Love conquers all. I believe that. If you and Joshua are meant to be together, it will work out, somehow."

"You've been brainwashed by those stupid romance novels you read, Elayne." Serenity wagged her finger. "Don't listen to her, CJ. He's not going to change his ways. He's infatuated with you—you're beautiful, fun, kind—what more could he want? Except you're not Amish. He won't change. Your heart will be broken."

Talk about different perspectives. I knew Serenity was just protecting me. I wondered why Elayne had such an optimistic viewpoint. Maybe she just wanted to sit back and enjoy the fireworks.

Serenity must have sensed that I was softening. She blurted out, "He'll have fun with you, CJ. But in the end, he'll marry a well-behaved Amish woman."

She was right. Serenity was always right.

But Elayne wasn't about to give up so easily. "That's hog wash. It's amazing you ever agreed to marry Daniel with such depressing ideas about love and romance." She tilted her head at me. "I can't make any promises about how it would turn out, but you don't have a lot of competition in the community. Most of the women past twenty-five are already happily married."

"There's a new woman in the settlement," I pointed out. "She looks to be about our age, and she's pretty, too."

"You must be talking about Rosetta Bontrager." I nodded confirmation and Elayne added, "She's a widow. Her husband was kicked in the chest by a horse he was training last year. They had only been married a few years and didn't have any kids. She waited a while to tie the knot—she's twenty-seven."

"How do you know all this stuff?" Serenity breathed.

"Think of it like one of your criminal investigations. I like to keep tabs on what's going on in the community I came from," Elayne admitted.

"Why is she here?" I asked, trying to sound casual.

"Looking for a new husband," Elayne drawled.

Serenity threw her hands up and gave me the, *I told you so* look.

"I don't understand," I muttered.

Elayne looked sympathetic. "Sometimes if a man or woman can't find someone they want to court in their own community, they'll travel to a neighboring settlement, or even a far-off destination, to make a match. Since Rosetta is older and a widow, it'll be more difficult for her to find a man with the right circumstances to pair up with her. She left her home in Pennsylvania to come to Blood Rock, Indiana." She motioned for me and Serenity to lean in and we did. "Someone in Blood Rock must have put out a notice that there was an eligible widower right here in our community. I can't see any other reason for her sudden appearance."

"A notice?" I said lamely.

"Not figuratively. More like a gossip line between the women and even some men to other communities. Even without modern technology, information gets passed along," Elayne said.

Serenity tapped her finger on the table. "Bingo! And there's our reason for the bishop allowing you to stay in the cottage, CJ." She leaned back and dropped her hands into her lap. "He doesn't think you're a threat anymore."

I turned to Elayne, and her expression had darkened. "That may be true, especially considering who Rosetta Bontrager is related to."

Serenity and I stared at Elayne, waiting for her to drop her little bombshell.

After Elayne must have deemed there was significant anticipation, and our attention was firmly directed at her, she said, "She's the bishop's niece."

6

JOSHUA

I gripped the porch railing and stared down the hill at the little white cottage that was nestled between two slopes and faced the lower field. CJ's car still hadn't returned. The sun had just dropped low on the distant rise, and the muted gray of twilight settled over the farm. A few birds still chirped, searching for branches to perch for the night, but otherwise the evening was still. With the absence of the sun, the air turned chilly. I welcomed the crisp touch on my bare arms. This was my favorite time of the year. When the days were still warm, but the nights cooled considerably, giving us a signal that autumn was right around the corner. Unfortunately, I couldn't enjoy the change of season. I was far too concerned with the whereabouts of an English woman to relax.

I filled my lungs with a large breath and closed my eyes. No, CJ wasn't just my tenant. She was much more than that.

The screen door creaked and Nora peeked out. "Dinner's ready, Da."

I nodded. "Is your sister still sleeping?"

"Yes—whatever the doctor gave her sure was good stuff," she replied.

I smiled at her choice of words. Just the short time my girls had spent with CJ that same day had affected their speech patterns. The realization made me alarmingly aware of how much influence she'd have on Nora and Sylvia if she was around too much. I pushed my hat back and rubbed my forehead. I didn't want CJ to leave, but what would happen if she stayed? The electricity that had popped between us earlier in the day gave me my answer. I had hoped that after a couple months away from each other, the attraction would have waned. But it had only gotten worse.

The resounding *clip clops* lifted my gaze to the road. I watched the buggy make its way along the road at a fast clip, only to slow at my driveway and turn in.

I recognized the horse. It belonged to Aaron Esch. My mind swirled at the reasons the bishop was paying me an unexpected visit.

I waited at the bottom of the steps for the buggy to come to a stop. The bishop wasn't alone.

"Good evening, Joshua. I hope we're not stopping by at a bad time," Aaron said when he stepped away from his horse.

Rosetta paused at the hitching rail. She offered a small nod in greeting.

"The meal is on the table. You arrived at just the right time," I assured him.

It was then that I noticed the tote in Rosetta's hands. She raised it up for me to see. "We worried about the little girl and wanted to check in on her. I brought snickerdoodle cookies."

My heart slowed as my gaze shifted to the bishop. Kids broke arms and legs throughout the community on a fairly regular basis. Such things didn't bring the bishop out. He was more concerned with sermons and making sure everyone behaved themselves. Aaron Esch wasn't being truthful. Something was on the wind.

I forced my voice to stay steady. "I hope you'll join us for supper."

"That would be welcomed," he replied. He attempted to smile, but the look was tight and unnatural.

Nana's expression when I came through the doorway with Aaron on my heels and Rosetta close behind him, would have made me laugh if I wasn't so uncomfortable with the arrival of the unanticipated guests.

"Aaron and Rosetta came by to check on Sylvia," I told her before she had a chance to ask.

Nana snorted. "Nice to see you again, Rosetta." She completely ignored Aaron.

It had come to light that the two had courted for a short time when they very young. Whatever happened between Nana and Aaron to make them quit each other was a mystery to me, but I'd learned almost immediately upon moving to the Blood Rock community that Nana didn't like the man one bit.

"Thank you for sharing the meal," Rosetta said curtly. She set the tote bag on the counter. "What do you need help with?"

Nana's hands were full with the pot of mashed potatoes. She thrust her chin out. "The dishes are over there. Can you put them on the table?"

"Of course." Rosetta hurried to her task. She was so slim in her blue frock that I doubted she ate very much. My mind drifted back to the tank top CJ had worn earlier. She was also a slender woman, but the curves of her breasts and hips were pronounced.

I blinked away the image and cleared my throat. "Excuse me." Rosetta inclined her head, but her expression didn't bely her thoughts. "I was just asking Nana about Laura's delivery," she told me and turned back to Nana. "I hope it went well."

"It was her sixth child. The baby practically slipped right out," Nana said gruffly.

Rosetta hid a smile behind her hand and Nora burst out laughing. I shot the girl a threatening look and she quickly quieted.

"Not very appropriate supper conversation, if you ask me, eh, Joshua?" Aaron said.

I nodded agreement and pulled out the chair for Aaron. He seated himself next to John, and dropped his head. Everyone followed suit for a silent prayer. I wasn't able to focus on speaking to God. The scurrying of movement alerted me prayer time had passed and I opened my eyes reluctantly.

Aaron and I dished out our food first, and then John. Once the boy had filled his plate with roasted beef, mashed potatoes, and baked summer squash, the females took their seats. It was a custom that had never given me much pause before, but as I listened to Nana and Rosetta chirp about Laura's new baby, I wondered what CJ would have thought about the men spooning out their food first. I shook the silent question away. I had to chase the woman from my thoughts.

"Have you gotten all your hay put up?" Aaron asked conversationally.

"I have. It's been a productive summer, but I'm looking forward to the quieter days to come."

"Autumn is my favorite time of the year. I enjoy canning and cooler weather," Rosetta said.

I glanced up at her. The resemblance to her uncle was noticeable. She was tall and lean. Her eyes were sharp, and her face foxlike. I had to admit, she was an attractive woman.

The conversation turned to the upcoming fall benefit dinner. It was an event held each year to raise money for our schoolhouse and teacher's salary. I tried to pay attention, but found myself inclining my head from time to time to listen for the sound of the approach of an automobile's engine.

I rose with Aaron after the meal, and was surprised when Rosetta spoke directly to me again. "Nana said you have some hens for sale. I'd like to take a look at them, if you don't mind."

Before I had the chance to respond, Aaron spoke up. "That's fine. I'll help Nana clean up."

I licked my lips. My heart was beating faster at the absurdity of it. I doubted Aaron had ever helped clean up a kitchen when visiting. The women took care of that, while the men retreated to the porch. It was obvious what the bishop was doing—he wanted Rosetta to have the opportunity to be alone with me. The idea of the old man trying his hand at matchmaking was ridiculous.

"I can take you to see the chickens," Nora spoke up.

"You stay and help your grandmother, child." Rosetta smiled easily. "I'd like to talk prices with your father."

Nora looked at me with her face scrunched in confusion. I had to play the game. If I didn't, my relationship with CJ would come into question. If that happened, I had no doubt the bishop would insist that I evict CJ.

I gestured toward the hallway. "Go check on Sylvia, Nora. If she's awake, come fetch me." I hoped Nora came running with news that Sylvia was indeed awake. That would give me the perfect reason to excuse myself from Rosetta's company.

I had to smile when I stepped out on the porch. The scowl on Nana's face told me she wasn't happy about the bishop inserting himself into her kitchen duties.

"It's a lovely evening." Rosetta matched my strides as we crossed the yard.

"It is," I mumbled.

The sun had disappeared behind the barn, and in its place was a pink and orange sky. I paused for a moment and stared. It was quite a sight.

Rosetta stood with me. She didn't say anything, just enjoyed the view.

I forced myself not to look when I finally heard a car pulling into the driveway. My limbs came to life, and I stretched my legs to reach the coop faster. I hoped CJ hadn't seen me with Rosetta.

"Here they are," I said briskly. "It's the barred rock hens"—I pointed—"there in the back, that are available."

I looked around. The barnyard was empty, except for the horses, cows, and chickens.

"You have a nice flock, Joshua," Rosetta said. She knelt to get a better look. "Are you willing to part with all of them?"

"Sure," I said, distracted. Was CJ angry with me for not allowing her to come into the hospital with us?

Rosetta straightened. Her look was gentle. "It's all right. You won't be judged for being out here alone with me. My uncle isn't my chaperone. I'm twenty seven years old and a widow, after all."

My mouth was dry. I risked meeting her gaze. "I'm sorry about your husband. Was it an accident?"

She nodded. "He was shoeing a young horse, a very rank and difficult beast. I had warned him to pass on the job, but he insisted he could work with the animal, train him to behave." She snorted softly. "The colt reared up, broke its lead line. While James was grabbing for the rope, the animal spun and kicked out, striking him squarely in the chest. I saw it happen."

"I'm sorry I brought it up…" I trailed off.

Her manner was business-like. "No worries. It's easier to talk about it now. He died a year ago in May.

We stood in awkwardly silence for a few moments. Rosetta was the one to speak first. "My uncle told me your wife died from an accident as well."

I gave the usual response when the subject was brought up. "Yes. She drowned when her buggy was swept into the river during a storm."

"It must be hard to raise three children on your own."

I shrugged, inhaling a long breath. "I wouldn't be able to do it without Nana's help," I admitted.

"How long have you been in Blood Rock?"

"Just a few months." I reluctantly met her gaze. She didn't look away. She was bolder than most Amish women.

"I hope you don't think I'm prying, but how come you moved here? I would think being surrounded by family and a community you knew well, would have been better than going to a new place, where you knew only a handful."

Her question was reasonable. I didn't hesitate. "There were too many reminders of my wife there. I thought it would be best for my family if we started over someplace new."

Her eyes were dark with curiosity. "Why pick Blood Rock? This community has had a lot of ill-happenings in recent years."

"Almost like the area is cursed?" I eyed the woman and she nodded in a friendly manner.

"Not exactly cursed, but you must admit this isn't the sleepy community you had probably hoped for."

"I've been around long enough to know there isn't a community anywhere that doesn't have its secrets." I breathed easier, finding it comfortable to talk to Rosetta. "If Blood Rock's past disturbs you, why are you here, then?"

"It doesn't bother me. You're right. There are dirty garments in everyone's closet. My own home is no different." She lifted her shoulders and her voice lightened. "Although, the murder rate seems higher here than most places I've visited."

"Are you on a tour of some kind?" I regretted my words. It sounded rude, but Rosetta took it in stride.

"Actually, I kind of am. When poor James died, I was distraught for a long while. We were just kids when we married as seventeen year olds." She leaned in and lowered her voice. I glanced over her head to see if anyone was watching. "You see, I was pregnant." I kept my face neutral, but my breathing slowed. "I'm sorry to shock you, but it is what it is. I'm not going to lie about anything to anyone. If you were to talk to the right person, you would have learned about my sins in time, anyway."

"It's a sin that many are guilty of." I pressed my lips together, but since she brought it up, I had to ask. "Where's your child?"

She was looking at the coop, but I could tell she wasn't seeing it at all. "A few weeks after the wedding, I miscarried. James and I weren't able to conceive after that."

I stepped back. The conversation was becoming uncomfortable.

"Do you think I'm too forward?" Her brows rose.

"No, not really. It's just I barely know you."

She nodded. "I've spent the past few months visiting relatives and friends in other communities to take my mind off my unfortunate state of affairs. I needed a break from the same faces. Many of them had passed judgment on me when James and I had rushed to get married. Everywhere I went was a constant reminder of what I had lost. I needed a change or I would have gone insane."

I offered a genuine smile. I knew exactly what she meant. "We're kind of in the same boat."

"Yes, we are," Rosetta said softly.

"I'm sorry to bother you, Mr. Miller."

I froze. It was CJ. She wore denim jeans and a gray cardigan sweater. Her hands were in the pockets and she hugged the material around her. The sun had set and a chill was in the air.

Her voice was brisk, but her face didn't give away her mood. She offered Rosetta a quick smile and turned to me. "The electricity isn't working in the house. I tried the breaker box, and that didn't fix it."

My head felt heavy. The most alluring woman I'd ever met stood before me, needing my help. I wanted to leave Rosetta and go immediately with CJ, but I knew how suspicious that would look.

"I have company, Ms. West. I'll be down in a little while to see if there's anything I can do. Electricity isn't my strong suit."

Her eyes narrowed. "I can call an electrician, no problem."

"No need for that, just yet." I worked hard to keep the edge out of my voice. Why did the beautiful woman have to be so difficult?

Rosetta interrupted. "It's fine, Joshua. Go help your tenant. I can only imagine how awful it is for an English woman to be without utilities."

I watched CJ's face go from annoyed to downright hostile in the blink of an eye. She spun around and marched down the hill to the cottage without another word.

"I hope I didn't offend her," Rosetta said.

She looked up at me with wide-eyed confusion, but I wasn't fooled. I had seen the fleeting look of satisfaction in her eyes.

"She's had a rough couple of months. Don't take her behavior personally." I tipped my hat. "You're welcome to come get the chickens whenever you want."

I was backing away from her when she followed me. "I enjoyed our chat. It was nice to speak freely for a change."

I forced my head to nod. "Yes. Yes, it was."

I turned and left Rosetta standing alone beside the coop—and I didn't look back. The fact that she was the bishop's niece complicated things. I didn't want to upset her. I knew how women could be. If I denied her outright, she might help convince Aaron and the other ministers that CJ had to go.

But getting CJ to understand my dilemma wouldn't be easy. Her mind didn't work like the women I'd grown up with. Although I'd never admit it out loud, that was one of the reasons I found her so appealing. She had a mind of her own, and that was refreshing.

I braced for CJ's temper when I crossed the driveway. I was ready for her to give me a hard time, but still, I couldn't wait to see her again.

7

CJ

I leaned against the old rock wall of the basement as Joshua fiddled around with the breaker box. Even though I didn't want to stare, I couldn't take my eyes off him. He had slim hips and wide shoulders. The suspenders over his blue shirt made him look like he'd just stepped out of a historical romance novel.

I blinked and averted my gaze when he faced me. He leaned in closer than was necessary to talk about the electrical problem. If I inhaled deeply, I was sure I would catch a whiff of his musky outdoorsy scent.

"I don't know what the problem is," he admitted.

"Are you sure you paid the bill?" I couldn't keep myself from smirking.

"Of course, I paid the bill. It's not that," he retorted. "I'll arrange for someone to come over and take a look at everything tomorrow."

"What am I supposed to do tonight? I don't have any lights, and the TV won't work."

His lips thinned. "I can provide you with candles and a lantern. It won't be too cold tonight. As long as you shut all your windows, the cottage should hold the heat. As far as not having the use of the television set, you could consider reading a book."

I grunted, and then chuckled. "Usually, I'd be reading anyway, but I'm binge watching a show and I hate to miss the next episode."

"Binge watching?" He looked truly perplexed.

"Never mind," I said and rolled my eyes.

A horse's hoof beats could be heard on the driveway. We both paused to listen.

The sound moved away as I held my breath. I climbed the steps back into the kitchen and opened the cupboard doors below the sink. I sensed Joshua was right behind me, but I didn't look up. I reached around until my fingers grasped a thick candle and I pulled it out.

I placed the candle on a plate and set it on the table. Then I rummaged through the miscellaneous drawer for the lighter. Joshua had one in hand when I turned back.

"Guess you always carry one for your gas lights." I plopped onto the chair and watched the dancing flame come to life.

"It comes with the territory." He took a seat across the table and folded his arms. "About earlier, I want to explain—"

I threw up my hands. "You don't have to say a thing. I get it. I'm just your tenant—or an occasional driver. It was presumptuous of me to think I'd be welcome to accompany you into the hospital with your injured daughter."

I tried to hide the look of hurt in my eyes by staring at the table top, focusing on the swirling grains of the wood. Joshua sighed loudly.

He lowered his voice, and the sound of him saying my name made warm honey spread through my insides.

"CJ...stop it."

I dared to raise my head. "Stop what—saying the truth?"

He moved his hands closer, but I snatched mine away.

"It would have looked unseemly if you had been with me and the girls in the hospital."

"No one would have cared, Joshua. None of your people were there."

He leaned further over the table. His face was tight with agitation. "You never know who might have been there. Just the other day one of the boys on a building crew accidently shot himself in the hand with a nail gun. He went to that very same hospital. Or a driver might be there for any number of reasons." There was quiet desperation in his voice. "We have to be careful."

"Why? So I can stay here forever? Won't my presence crimp your style with the pretty, new Amish woman?" I feared I had snarled the words out. I took a calming breath and folded my hands on my lap, leaning back.

Joshua's mouth dropped open and then snapped shut. He shook his head vigorously. "Rosetta has nothing to do with anything at all," he insisted.

I pursed my lips and stared at him. The corner of his mouth twitched and I suddenly wanted to kiss him badly. It was a terrible feeling.

"You can go now. I have enough candles to get me through the night. And the food should be all right in the refrigerator if I don't open the door very much." I stood and gripped the back of the chair. "Please, just go."

"Is that what you really want?" His eyes looked troubled.

"You've already made that decision for us. We have to start acting like we're simply landlord and tenant." I nodded my head. "If we have to move on, then we might as well start now."

Joshua grabbed his hat from off the table and left without saying goodbye.

I slumped back into the chair and pressed my face into my hands. It was for the best, I knew, but it still felt like my heart was breaking all over again.

My cellphone vibrated and I snatched it off the counter. It was a message from Serenity.

It read—I HOPE YOU DON'T MIND, I GAVE ELAYNE YOUR NUMBER. YOU NEED SOME FUN!

"What the heck," I muttered, staring at the phone.

The phone rang. It was a private number. "Hello?" I said slowly.

"Are you ready for a girls' night out?" It was Elayne.

"Did Serenity put you up to this?"

Elayne giggled wickedly. "I never need persuasion for a drink at Charlie's Pub."

"I'm sorry. I'm kind of tired—" There was a knock at the door.

I picked up the plate with the candle and made my way to the front door, still holding my cellphone to my ear. When I opened the door, I was shocked to see Elayne standing on the other side. She waved her phone in the air and her smile stretched from ear to ear. Her long black hair was down and her heels were no shorter than four inches. The little black dress she had on made me instantly jealous.

Anticipation bubbled up into my throat. I'd probably hate myself in the morning, but a couple of drinks and some female company was definitely what I needed at the moment. Anything to get my mind off Joshua Miller.

"It'll take me a few minutes to get ready."

"Take your time. I want you to look good," Elayne said.

I raised my brow and she laughed at me. "There's no conspiracy, CJ. I just don't want people to think I have frumpy friends. That's one of the reasons I left the Amish."

Maybe I was too paranoid.

"Why is it so dark?" Elayne asked as she followed me into the bedroom.

"Power's out in the house."

"Then I really did rescue you from a difficult evening."

You have no idea how true that is, Elayne, I thought.

8

JOSHUA

My legs were heavy as I walked down the hallway to the room shared by Sylvia and Nora. The house was dark and quiet. Nana had already retired to her bedroom and I'd checked in on John, who was sound asleep. I pushed the girls' door open and went straight to the open window. Cold air was shooting through the crack, and I quickly lowered the window and then latched it closed. The sky was clear and starry. As I paused, looking out, my gaze was drawn to the cottage. CJ's car was there, but she wasn't. I'd seen a vehicle pull up the driveway earlier and I'd heard women's voices. They had left together a few minutes later.

I inhaled deeply and blew out a long breath, fogging up the glass. I was the one who had told CJ that we couldn't have a relationship, but each and every time I was near the woman, doubts crept in. With every step I took, I thought of her, and my nights were long and sleepless. If pushing CJ away was the right thing to do, why did I feel so awful?

"Da?" cooed Sylvia.

I crossed the floor and sat on the bed beside her. She raised her head and yawned. "Is it morning?"

"No, baby. It's still nighttime." I pushed her tangles aside and rubbed her cheek. "How do you feel?"

"My arm don't hurt anymore. Will you sign my cast, too?" She pointed. "Look, Nora, John, and Nana already did."

I leaned in closer. "That's really neat. Yes, I'll add my name when the sun comes up," I promised.

Sylvia pouted up at me. "Nora said that tall woman stopped by with the bishop."

"Yes, she brought you cookies."

"I don't like her. She's bossy," Sylvia said.

I smiled in the dark. I kind of agreed with her about Rosetta, but I couldn't tell the child that. "You mustn't say mean things, Sylvia. She came here to check on you. That was nice of her."

"Is she going to be our...new ma?" Sylvia's voice trembled.

Nora suddenly rolled over on her bed, covering her head with the blanket. I snorted, and spoke loud enough that my older daughter, who was feigning sleep, could hear. "My goodness, why would you ask such a question? I only met the woman today."

"Nora says that's why she came over—not to see me, but to get her claws into you."

I threw my head back and grunted. It was fascinating how perceptive children could be. Nora was only ten years old, and already, she understood womanly behavior quite well. As impressed as I was with my daughter's intuition, this was a serious matter.

"Nora, I know you're awake. Come over here," I ordered in a stern voice.

Sylvia's eyes went wide. Nora tossed the blanket back and climbed out of the bed. She made her way slowly over and stopped before me. Her feet were bare and her little toes curled down. She lifted her head and bravely met my gaze.

"Ms. Bontrager stared at you the entire meal. Didn't you see?" Nora implored.

I worked hard to keep from smiling. "You're mistaken, Nora. Rosetta's a friendly woman, and she's visiting a new community. She wants to meet people."

"I heard Mrs. Bachman and Mrs. Yoder talking yesterday at the barn raising. They were saying Ms. Bontrager is looking for a husband, and that's why she's here."

The desire to burst into laughter was great, but I held my face steady. "It's not nice to eavesdrop. I won't have you spying on your elders," I raised my hand to stop the child's interruption. Nora could be very insolent. "I will have no more talk of this. Do you hear me, Nora?" She slowly nodded, but her mouth was still firmly set. "Rosetta Bontrager is only a friend. Do not start gossip about things you do not understand." I nudged her toward her bed. "Now off to sleep you go. Tomorrow is a big day."

"Can I still go to the schoolhouse dinner, Da?" Sylvia asked. Her eyes were round and desperate.

"Of course. Now that you have your arm casted, you can do many things." I leaned over and kissed her forehead.

"Even chores? Doctor said I should be careful." Sylvia yawned again.

I chuckled. "Well, if you're in fine enough shape to go to the schoolhouse, I'd think you could manage to help your sister with a few of the chores—like gathering the eggs and feeding your rabbits."

She beamed. "Oh, yes. I can still do those things."

Nora grumbled as she climbed into bed. I pulled the covers up under her chin and was turning away when she bolted upright.

"Don't you like CJ anymore?" Nora asked.

Her wild-eyed look bothered me. I took a deep breath. "Of course, I like CJ. She's a kind woman."

"Isn't she still our friend?" she pestered.

I forced a patient look. "Why, dear Nora, are you asking such questions?"

"You were mean to her today. She drove us to the hospital, and she wanted to come in with us, but you made her leave."

The child was right, but it would be many more years before she'd truly understand why I turned CJ away. For now, I had to do my best to settle her mind on the subject.

"CJ is our friend, but don't forget she's English. That means we can only have so much contact with her. It might seem unfair, but it's for the best that we don't get accustomed to spending too much time with her. Otherwise, someday when she leaves, you girls will be very sad."

"Will you miss her, Da?" Nora asked.

The question was innocent and straightforward, but it made me stiffen. I stood and headed for the door.

"Say your prayers, girls, and go to sleep," I ordered.

When their bedroom door was shut behind me, I leaned back against it and closed my eyes.

Finally answering Nora's question, I mumbled to myself. "Yes, I will miss CJ, more than you'll ever know."

9

CJ

I took a swig of the draft beer in front of me, and tapped my foot to the music. Elayne was sipping something a lot stronger. Charlie's Pub was full of happy people. I fixed a fake smile on my face and pretended to be one of them.

"Oh, come on." Elayne purred. "Surely, you're enjoying yourself?"

I shrugged a little. I didn't want to be rude. "Yeah, it's nice to go out and be among the living again."

Elayne leaned in. "It must have been horrible what you went through." She swallowed a large sip of her drink. "I'm not sure if I would be in as good of shape as you are right now."

"My ribs still hurt, but not as bad as they did."

She snorted softly. "I wasn't talking about your body, CJ. I meant your mind." She paused and glanced around the pub, her eyes darting over the crowd. "I'm completely paranoid now. I knew Caleb Johnson in passing. He was one of the Amish drivers, so I saw him on occasion. It still blows my mind what he did to those poor girls." Her face paled and she took another drink. "He used to come in here all the time, and I never guessed he was a freak."

I lowered my voice, even though the music was blaring. "You knew one of the girls, didn't you?"

She had a faraway look on her face. "Hannah Kuhns was living with me when she went missing. She wanted to leave the Amish. I was helping her do just that."

"Why did she want to leave?"

"Like me when I was that age, Hannah had her wild oats to sow. She was independent in nature. She wanted to go to college and get a nursing degree. She couldn't stand wearing the dresses, and being told what to do by the Amish authority. Poor Hannah had one shot at staying Amish and he was taken from her in a terrible way."

"He?"

"Eli Bender was her beau. He was killed when a crazy woman created a gas leak and blew up the house he was in. Didn't Serenity mention it?"

"No, can't say that I remember her talking about it," I replied with a shiver.

"Hannah went through a lot. Once Eli was gone, that girl was ready to leave. She was just biding her time until she had her ducks in a row, but she never made it out."

"Is it really that bad—being Amish, I mean."

Elayne took another swig from her glass. "I miss it sometimes, I was close to my sisters and mother, but when I left, those relationships changed forever. I still see them sometimes, but it's usually tense. Ma will never forgive me for leaving. She's polite, but that's it."

"Are there other things you miss?"

Her expression changed. She looked like a cat, flicking her tail. "Well, I enjoyed baking and gardening with my sisters. It's the female companionship I miss. When I was Amish, I was never alone. I had family and friends who were always there for me. The outside world can be a lonely place."

"What about the men?" Her eyes widened, and I quickly added, "Did you have someone special you liked?"

She frowned slightly. "Actually, I was pretty sweet on Daniel Bachman, Serenity's fiancé."

My face must have shown my shock, because she laughed. "Nothing happened, trust me. He wasn't as interested in me as I was in him. It's funny, though, that we both eventually went English."

"I hope I'm not bothering you with a bunch of nosey questions," I paused, looking for the right words. "I'm just trying to understand Joshua and his family better."

She arched a brow. "I get it." She drew back. "Ask away."

"There are a lot of people in the community and they seem content. What made you leave, Elayne?"

"There are hundreds of thousands of Amish people across the United States. Because their settlements are large and spread out, most people don't realize how many of us"—she smiled, correcting herself—"them, there really are." She tilted her head. "I always had a problem with authority. Out of all of my siblings, I was the rebellious one—the child who asked too many questions and argued about all the answers."

She flashed a smile, but her mind was elsewhere. "I loved to read, too. My mother was quite lenient in that department, and we'd go to the Blood Rock library on a weekly basis. She didn't always peruse my reading material, and it was there, in that library, that I began to learn about the outside world. I read about faraway, foreign lands, and strong, independent women. The seed was planted, and as I grew, I became more and more resentful about my life. Most of my time was taken up doing chores and house cleaning, and hardly any in the classroom. Like all the other Amish children, my school days were over when I finished eighth grade. I was only thirteen at the time. My workload picked up, and my parents insisted I begin cleaning neighbors' houses with my sisters for extra income. I also baby sat for an English family up the road, and cared for my own younger siblings. Nearly all of my earnings were turned over to my parents, and it would have stayed that way until I was engaged. Besides putting in full work weeks at that young age, I also helped my mother with the household chores, laundry, and cooking. I was exhausted much of the time."

I had to interrupt her. "How do Amish parents get away with taking their kids' income? I would think they'd all revolt—and how is it legal that you only went to school until eighth grade?"

She sighed softly. I got the impression she'd told this story before, and had already answered the same questions a million times.

"As far as the income goes, it's tradition. The Amish have large families, and when their children finish school, they go into the workforce. A percentage of the family's income comes from the money that's brought in from the teenagers. Those same children know that when they have their own family one day, they'll receive the same benefit from their kids. Once the young people reach nineteen or twenty, if they're not already married, they're allowed to keep more of their income. That way they can begin their own family."

"Archaic," I muttered under my breath, but Elayne heard.

"Yes, but it really does work. Rarely do Amish families have financial troubles, and it's readily accepted by parents and children alike."

"Except you and Daniel," I commented.

"You're right. I didn't like giving my hard-earned money to my parents. I had plans in my mind of better uses for it. I'm sure Daniel was the same way." She emptied her glass with a gulp. "As far as the education situation goes, it works as well. It gives teens the ability to enter the workforce at an earlier age, thus bringing more money into the household." She raised her hand when I was about to interrupt her. "Amish youth learn trades from family and friends, like welding, building houses, and farming. They develop those skills at a young age, and become masters at their trade in the process. It's also our first amendment right, you know—freedom of religious expression. That's how the Amish can govern themselves."

"What about the girls? Hmm? They don't become builders and farmers, do they?" I couldn't keep the venom from my voice.

"No, no, they don't. They take those years between school age and marriage to learn how to manage a house and large family properly. They cook, clean, and care for their younger siblings. They garden, learn to can food, quilt, sew, and do bookkeeping for their future husband's business. Oftentimes, wives are equal partners in a family business. Although, when the babies start coming, they don't have a lot of time for it."

"That is sickening," I breathed.

Elayne stiffened. "I agree, and that's why I left. Unlike my sisters, I didn't have a beau that rocked my world. All I had was hot resentment that I couldn't have a career, like the women in the novels I read. I wanted to go to a large university to become a doctor—that's what I initially wanted to do. It wasn't until my second year of college that I changed my major to law. I decided that I was more suited to helping people by being an advocate for justice, rather than sewing them back up."

"How did you escape?" I studied Elayne over the rim of my mug.

"It was the hardest thing I ever did, really. I was eighteen, and had thought about leaving many times during the previous few years. I only got my nerve up to actually do it when one of my ma's own sisters came for a quick visit. She had gone English fifteen years earlier. She stopped by one sunny summer afternoon to have tea with Ma. They had continued to talk, even though my aunt was officially shunned by the community. I made up my mind that day, and when my aunt got into her car to drive away, I jumped into her vehicle and begged her to take me with her. I think my mother might have already talked to her sister about me, and the problems I was having with the lifestyle. Maybe that's why she came for a visit in the first place. All that mattered is that she said yes, and I left my family that day with only the simple smock on my back and the black shoes on my feet."

I ordered another beer from the waitress and settled into the chair, letting Elayne's story sink in. We were silent for a minute before I finally woke from my thoughtful trance. "Your parents never came looking for you?"

Elayne shook her head rapidly. "They knew it was best for me—and for them. Mother and Father didn't want me corrupting my other siblings with ideas of education and travel. They had nine children. Losing me wasn't a big deal."

"I can't imagine giving birth to nine kids…"

She grinned. "Eleven—after I left, Ma had twins."

I sipped on my newly arrived beer. I was comfortable talking to Elayne. She'd just bared her heart wrenching life to me. Even though she wore four-inch spiked heels, a tiny dress, and looked like a super-model, she was still somehow relatable. I sympathized with her childhood plight. In order to have the life she wanted, she had to leave her family behind. Most girls would have accepted their fate, married a cute boy, and remained Amish. That would have been the simplest route—but Elayne Weaver hadn't taken the easy road. She'd left everything she knew behind and went to college, eventually becoming a lawyer and the assistant district attorney of Blood Rock. I wondered if a part of her regretted her decision. She was my age, early thirties I guessed—and she wasn't married and had no kids. She was alone, like me. Was she truly happy?

I glanced up and watched her stare at the small stage where the band played. She tapped her finger on the table. I wouldn't ask her about regrets. After all, no matter what choices we made in life, we all were bound to have some disappointments.

Her words had opened my eyes to the challenges Joshua faced. If he left the Amish, then his kids would be forced out, too. How could he make that decision for them? And he seemed perfectly content with his restricted lifestyle. I was being selfish to think he would ever leave his world to be with me.

I set the tumbler down a little too hard and Elayne's head snapped my way.

"You really do have it bad for Joshua Miller, don't you?" she asked.

Normally, I would have been annoyed at the question, but she had been open and honest with me. I felt an obligation to do the same with her. "I won't lie, there's a very strong attraction there, and I think he feels the same way about me. He made it clear today that it would never work out between us. Joshua's terrified of his community finding out that we...well...like each other. If that happens, I'll be promptly evicted, and he would get into trouble. Yet, even though he doesn't want me around, he doesn't seem to want me to leave, either."

There was a hint of vexation in her tone. "Joshua's in a rough place. He's one of our people who truly enjoys being Amish. I did the paperwork for the closing on his farm here in Blood Rock. His eyes absolutely twinkled when he talked about farming and how his son had the same bug for it he had. He gushed about his daughters and how he thought they'd someday make a good match in this new community. I don't think he'd be happy living in the outside world."

"I know," I agreed quietly.

"Would you ever become Amish?"

The question nearly knocked me back in the chair. "Are you kidding?"

Her smile was small and knowing. "Oh, come on, I don't believe you haven't at least thought about that possibility."

"It never occurred to me that it was even possible," I admitted.

"It doesn't happen very often, but occasionally, an Amish person and an Englisher fall in love. They have two choices, basically. They can be English together—or they can be Amish. Usually, the couple will go English. It's just so much easier. I've noticed that when relationships like that happen, the Amish person was already living with a rebellious spirit. Sometimes the Englisher will become Amish. Trust me, it's not an easy path. There's a lot more sacrifices to be had when converting to the Amish than the other way around, but I've seen it happen."

I snorted loudly. "I can't imagine doing that. It would feel so phony—like I was pretending to be something I wasn't just so I could explore a relationship with a guy."

Elayne gave me the, *I really, really understand what you're saying* look. "I don't know you well, CJ, but believe it or not, there are a lot of women who'd be content living the Amish lifestyle if it meant having a good husband like Joshua, a few beautiful children, and a gorgeous farm to live on. I wasn't sure where you fell on the domestic housewife scale." She giggled and my eyes shot skyward. When she sobered, she added, "Seriously, though. I hate to see people who are in love throw it all away because of cultural differences."

"Relationships are hard when you come from the same background. Not driving cars or using electricity is a huge difference in lifestyle. Not to mention the dress code and having a handful of old men telling you what to do. If I were Amish, I'd probably kill someone," I insisted.

She held up her nearly empty glass. "To miracles, then," she knocked her glass to my mug.

Before we had a chance to lower our drinks, a man walked up to our table. I guessed he was our age. He was clean shaven and wearing a button up flannel shirt, blue jeans, and cowboy boots. I knew him. He worked on Daniel's building crew and Serenity had introduced us briefly at the diner one of the days before I was attacked. At that time, she'd advised me that I'd be a stupid fool if I didn't let the guy take me out to dinner. I had blushed and declined that day. Joshua Miller had been raging on my mind, and I'd completely dismissed the handsome newcomer.

"Hi, Elayne." He quickly turned to me and offered his hand. "CJ West, right?"

I tried to smile back, but I was flustered. "Yes, that's me. I'm surprised you remembered my name. I'm sorry"—I looked to Elayne for rescue—"I'm not so good with names."

"This is Nathan Hammond," Elayne said. Her brows rose high and a ghost of a smile touched her lips.

"Oh, yes. That's right." I shook his hand. He had a strong grip. "Nice to see you again," I said lamely.

His face tensed. "How are you feeling?"

Of course, he knew all about me being kidnapped and nearly murdered by a serial killer. Why wouldn't he?

"I'm doing well. Thanks for asking."

Elayne motioned to the empty chair. "Why don't you join us, Nathan?"

He smiled politely and I noticed the dimple at the corner of his mouth. "I won't impose on girl time." He shrugged. "Besides, I need to get home. I have an early morning appointment with a plumber."

He was about to pivot away when he stopped. His gaze rested on me. "Do you still live in the Amish community?" I nodded. My heart felt like it would break loose from my chest. "Are you going to the benefit dinner at the schoolhouse tomorrow evening?"

I looked at Elayne for clarification about what he was even talking about. She went a step further, and completely lied. "Yes, as a matter of fact, we were just talking about it. Best food of the year." She winked at me.

"That's great. Maybe I can sit with you." The side of Nathan's mouth lifted. "I always feel kind of funny at the Amish events—but I do love the food and it's for a good cause. It will be nice to have someone to hang out with."

I smiled back weakly, unable to say anything.

"Goodnight, ladies. Enjoy your evening," Nathan said.

When he was gone, I hissed, "What were you thinking saying I was going to schoolhouse! That was the first time I even heard about it." I rambled on. "Frankly, being around the Amish right now is not something I really want to do."

"You should be thanking me," Elayne said stiffly. "First off, you'll get a wonderful meal. Second, you will have the opportunity to spend an evening with an attractive and available non-Amish man."

"Why aren't you interested in him?" I challenged.

"I'm a little too high maintenance for Nathan. He's a country boy at heart, but since you seem to like that sort of thing, he might be right up your alley."

I gripped my head between my hands and moaned. "I'm not ready to go on a sorta-kinda date thing—and Joshua might be there."

Elayne's expression was smug. "Exactly! What better way to irritate the hell out of your landlord—the man who pushed you away—than to be seen spending time with another man? Hmm?"

I hated to admit that the workings of her diabolical mind were right on track. Besides, Joshua was already spending time with a pretty Amish woman. Why shouldn't I do the same?

I bobbed my head to the music and ordered another round for us. If I was going to survive a possible breaking heart, I had to occupy my time with painting and other adventures.

This time when I raised my drink and bumped Elayne's glass, I truly meant to enjoy myself.

After the past couple of months, I really did deserve a little bit of fun.

10

JOSHUA

Thick clouds stretched across the darkening gray sky. I could smell rain in the air. Leaves pelted the side of the tent when the breeze picked up, striking the canvas with a thousand taps. Hot air puffed up from the giant grill into my face, and I wiped the sweat off my forehead with the back of my free hand. My other hand was busy grasping the fork, and turning the roasting chicken legs.

"Where is Nicolas Swarey, anyway? He signed up for this job, not me," I huffed.

Lester Lapp placed some fresh chicken onto the grill. "Reckon, I don't know. The man's been more distant than usual lately. I've hardly seen him since his wife left."

I didn't much like Nicolas Swarey. He had devious eyes and an unfriendly nature, but up until today, I didn't have any personal grievances with the man. That had changed when Lester pulled me aside when I stepped out of my buggy, asking for my help with the grilling. I had agreed, but it soured my already ill mood even further. I yawned into my sleeve, remembering how I'd been up until two o'clock in the morning, waiting for CJ to return home. I had no idea where she'd gone, or why she'd gotten back to the cottage so late. There was no way I could fall asleep knowing that she was out there somewhere, especially after what had happened to her last summer. I shook my head a little, trying to clear my tired mind. I'd also had an early morning separating the calves and feeding the horses. By the look of the crowd lining up at the far end of the schoolhouse doors, it would be a long evening.

The trilling voice of the auctioneer sparked the air, and I paused my hand over the charcoals to listen. From the amounts being shouted out, I guessed the team of ponies that Joseph Bender donated were being sold. I snorted. I would have liked to have watched them in the ring.

"Thanks for coming to my aid, Joshua." Lester dug into the cooler for more chicken. Every time we filled a tub with roasted meat, one of the women snatched it away, hustling back to the food line.

My shoulders dropped. "Ah, no worries. It's probably best I'm not in the auction barn. I don't need any more horses or ponies."

Lester laughed. "Or furniture. Did you see the table and chairs Moses brought in? He really outdid himself this year."

"Naw. You grabbed me straight out of the buggy, remember? I never had a chance to walk through the building to see what was collected for the auction." I tried to keep my voice neutral.

"Then I saved you a fortune." Lester slapped my back. "The quilt the women are raffling off is a really fine work of art. I wouldn't be surprised if it brought over a thousand dollars."

"Nana enjoyed working on it. She finally feels comfortable with the other women." I glanced over. "She wasn't thrilled about leaving our old community. It's been a difficult adjustment for her."

"How about you, Joshua?" Lester's dark eyes were full of questions. "How do you feel about the move, now that you've been here a few months?"

I slowed my ministrations over the grill. "It hasn't been easy for me, either. At first, the children missed their friends, and the different rules here in Blood Rock took some time getting used to. But I think we've settled in all right, everything considered."

"And what about your lady tenant?" Lester asked.

When I looked up, his face was open and curious.

I liked Lester. He had been one of the first to welcome us into the community. He was fairly laidback, and easy to along with, too.

"Truth be told, I was shocked to learn it was a woman who had rented the cottage. Her brother was the one who had talked to me on the phone. I just assumed CJ West was a man."

"It's an honest mistake. Outsiders don't understand our customs. They don't even think about the same things we do. It probably never occurred to the brother that an unmarried English woman wouldn't be allowed to rent from you."

"She had all her luggage with her. I felt terrible telling her to leave. It just didn't seem right."

A boy ran up to Lester and asked him a question. He answered quickly and shooed the child away. "Looks like they're running low on chicken again."

"We can only cook the meat so quickly." I shook my head.

"How are things going, now that the elders have given their blessing to the woman remaining your tenant?" Lester's voice was low. He didn't want anyone to overhear our conversation.

Even if Lester was a close friend, I couldn't mention the real problem with having CJ on my property. She was a temptation I simply couldn't resist. "I'm not really sure it's for the best. CJ has been through a lot, you know, but my girls adore her, and that scares me."

Lester mumbled, "You don't want an Englisher to have too much influence on your children. That's trouble waiting to happen, if you ask me."

I pressed my lips together. "I fear you're right."

"Hello, Joshua." Rosetta had snuck up behind me.

I tipped my hat. "Good evening. Did you enjoy the dinner?"

"I waited for you," she said boldly.

Lester's eyes widened and he covered the broad grin on his face with his hand.

I recovered quickly. "I'm sorry to say, I'll be tied up with the grilling until dark. Best you go get your food."

"I'll take over from here, Joshua," the bishop said. He appeared at his niece's side at just the right moment.

"You don't have to do that. I volunteered to help Lester." I wiped my brow again with my sleeve. "It's an awfully hot job."

"Nonsense. In the early days of our community, I handled most of the grilling. I rather enjoy the mindless work." The bishop sidled up next to me and extended his hand for the fork.

My gaze darted between Lester and the bishop, but Lester remained silent.

I handed the utensil over and pulled the apron over my head. "It's all yours."

As we left the tent and headed to the back of the line, Rosetta glanced over and said, "It looked like you needed a break."

Rosetta's expression was friendly. Because of her unusual height, we were almost eye to eye. It was odd to have a woman at my side who was nearly as tall as me. Her hands were clasped in front of her and she swayed when she walked, giving me the impression she didn't have a care in the world. She was a unique woman, and I was sure that if CJ hadn't come into my life, I would have been interested in getting to know Rosetta better. Guilt prickled my skin that she had sought me out. I didn't want to hurt her feelings, but I wasn't ready for a relationship with anyone. I just couldn't do that to CJ. It was too soon.

Rosetta smiled and made small pleasantries with almost every woman we passed. For just arriving in the community, she was already quite popular. Being the bishop's niece helped, but I deemed her outgoing manner to be the main reason she had been so readily accepted. Life with a woman like her would be easy. She might have had a wild hair at a younger age, but as a grown woman, she'd accepted our ways and seemed genuinely happy to be Amish. I should be honored that the bishop was even trying to push the two of us together. Or that she was even interested in me.

A rumble in the distance turned our heads.

"Looks like a storm is coming," Rosetta said.

Ominous clouds were billowing to the west. The wind gusted and the flaps on the tent flipped up. Most of the tables and benches were full, and my attention strayed to the poles securing the large tent to the ground.

Rosetta followed my gaze. "Do you think it's safe enough?"

A small group of children ran by, squealing and calling out to each other. For a moment, Rosetta and I were separated. One of the girls was my very own Nora. Her lips pursed together when she saw who I was with. I ignored her sour-mouthed look.

"Where's Sylvia?" I shouted after her.

"She's eating with Nana in the kitchen," she called over her shoulder, not bothering to slow.

Rosetta stepped back into place. "That child is threatened by me."

Her words jerked my head in her direction. I didn't think she'd even recognized my older daughter in the crowd, let alone notice her frowning face.

"Nora is aloof. It takes her a while to get to know new people. I'm sure she'll come around in time."

She was satisfied with my reply. The corner of her mouth raised high. "Some of the ladies and their children are hiring a driver to take them to the zoo next week. Would you mind if your girls came with me?"

I hesitated. Before I responded, she quickly added, "It would give me a chance to become their friend."

The breeze picked up and I had to hold my hat on my head to keep it from catching the wind. "I don't think it will work out so soon. With Sylvia's broken arm and all, more of the chores have fallen on Nora's shoulders." She stared at the ground. I could tell she was fighting not to look disappointed. Once again, I found myself wanting to protect her feelings. "I'll keep it in mind though, if something changes."

She nodded as we ducked through the doorway into the school-house. It was nice to be out of the wind, and we both let out sharp breaths at the same time. Our eyes met, and we laughed. We were pressed closer together as we moved up in the line, nearing the food tables. To anyone watching, we would have looked like a courting couple. Well, at our age, more like a married pair. Our people didn't wear wedding rings, so there was no clear indication that a person was taken, except the beard on a man's face. Since I was a widower, I still kept mine long.

Our entrance into the school hadn't gone unnoticed. A lot of eyes paused on us. People were already speculating on the wedding day, I reckoned.

"Anything wrong?" Rosetta asked. Her expression was innocent, but I knew better. She was aware that we were being watched by everyone. Unlike the inner panic I was feeling, she was quite relaxed.

I shook my head and focused on the food. I picked up a plate and had the serving girls load it up with drumsticks, mashed potatoes, noodles, and green beans. The delicious aroma made my stomach growl. I hadn't eaten since breakfast.

We made our way back out of the building and over to the tent, where a family slid further down the bench to make room for us. Drops of rain began to tap against the roof. I looked out the flaps. People were beginning to run for cover.

Rosetta leaned into my shoulder. "Here it comes."

She was referring to the downpour, but my gaze caught a glimpse of someone, and my eyes flew open wider. I craned my neck to see over the hats and caps better.

It was CJ. She was running for the schoolhouse—and she wasn't alone.

11

CJ

I stood beside my car and stared at the sea of colorful dresses and long beards. There must have been a hundred people milling around the schoolhouse. A line of horses was tied to the fence, and a dozen buggies were stalled on the small gravel road leading to the parking area behind the school. A mixture of cars, pickup trucks, and buggies filled the grassy field. It was such a strange juxtaposition that I had to stop and digest scene.

Four little Amish girls streaked by. Their polyester dresses flapped in the wind. A brown dog trotted up and sniffed my hand, but when I tried to touch its head, it darted away. In the distance, I saw Katherine and Rebecca. They each carried a toddler in their arms and walked through the doorway into the school.

I stuck my hands in my pockets and looked up. Wind gusted into my face and the clouds were ringed with dark edges. I thought about grabbing the umbrella from the backseat, but hesitated. No one else had one, and I was afraid my giant purple umbrella might scare the horses.

Why was I here again? The side of my head throbbed slightly and

I pressed my fingers to the spot. I was getting too old for late night drinking adventures. A smile crept up on my lips. After Elayne and I had discussed all the serious matters that plagued us, we'd loosened up and had gotten out on the dance floor. A few beers had definitely helped me come out of my shell. I needed a distraction, and Elayne had happily provided just that.

I wasn't sure how Nathan Hammond had talked me into mingling with the neighbors though. The alcohol had definitely contributed to my decision, but there was also something very genuine and a little bit shy about the man that made me not want to disappoint him. Plus, I had a hard time saying no, something that had caused me to end up in a lot of places where I didn't really want to be.

Seeing the huge crowd, I was having second thoughts. A drop of rain splattered my nose and I wiped it away. It was a good excuse to head home, I decided.

I turned and nearly bumped into Nathan.

"Hello, there." His smile was knowing. "You weren't about to bail on me, were you?"

My heart stammered and I caught my breath. My cheeks were hot. "Of course not. I was thinking about my umbrella. Do you think it might scare the horses?"

Nathan looked thoughtfully at the horses tied to the fence. He was once again wearing denim jeans and a flannel shirt, although this one was green and brown. The colors matched his sandy-colored hair and tan complexion. He wasn't as tall as Joshua, but his shoulders were just as broad. He was a fine-looking man in the light of day, and minus influence of the beer too, thankfully.

"It might be best not to use one. Most of these horses have probably experienced just about everything, but you never know about one like that—" he nodded toward a spirited looking animal being ridden by a young boy. The horse hopped sideways and tossed his head. "The kid looks like an excellent rider, but we wouldn't want to contribute to a possible accident."

He had taken care not to tell me what to do, coaxing me instead. I liked his approach. Since I had only used the umbrella as an excuse to get out of Dodge, I readily agreed with him. "Good call. I'll leave it in my car."

Nathan glanced up. "We better hurry. Looks like we're in for a downpour." He pointed at the dark clouds massing above us. The temperature dropped a few degrees and I felt the chill of the oncoming rain.

I zipped my sweater up, dug my hands into the pockets, and headed in the direction of the schoolhouse doors, which seemed like a great distance now that raindrops pelted my head. The last thing I needed was for my natural curls to get wet and frizzed out like a bad eighties' hairdo.

Nathan matched my long strides and leaned over. "They are kind of intimidating, aren't they?"

I looked up. There were some non-Amish in sight, but most of the people coming and going from the building were Amish. I was getting used to seeing the black coated men with their long beards and the women in their Easter egg colored dresses, but when the entire community came together, it was an unusual sight. The horses and buggies only added to the surreal feeling.

"At first they were, but I've gotten used to them," I lied.

He grunted. "I like horses and all, but I can't imagine going without my truck."

I smiled sideways. "Yep. I'd have a hard time giving up my car, too."

The raindrops multiplied. Nathan grabbed my hand and tugged me forward. "We're not going to make it!"

He sounded as excited about the storm as a little boy would.

When I glanced over my shoulder, I saw the sheet of water coming toward us. I picked up my pace and shouted, "Run!"

We burst through the doors, wet and out of breath. I quickly scrunched my curls with my hand, silently praying that my conditioner would hold up to the onslaught.

"You're fast," Nathan breathed. He shook his head, and more water sprayed me.

"Hey, stop that," I said.

He mumbled an apology, but grinned the entire time as he ushered me into the food line. Wind battered the side of the building and there was no visibility through the rain-streaked windows. A clap of thunder shook the schoolhouse. I jumped and then shivered.

"Are you cold?" Nathan moved in closer.

"Not really. I love rain, but I hate storms like this." I crossed my arms and rubbed my forearms. "I guess I worry too much."

"Nonsense." Nathan handed me a heavy-duty plastic dinner plate. The delicious scents wafting from the counter drew my attention away from the storm. "It's smart to be cautious in this kind of weather." He leaned in. "Personally, I think it's a perfect type of night to stay home and watch a movie."

I almost laughed. "I was actually just thinking the same thing."

We talked about our favorite shows while the Amish girls dished out our food. I had a hard time deciding between the peanut butter and cherry pies, but in the end, I chose the peanut butter crème and a scoop of homemade vanilla ice cream.

My mouth watered as I followed Nathan around a group of teenage girls. I listened to their brisk talking as we passed by, and wondered if there was a book about the language I could study. Nathan steered me through the doors and right under the tent. A dozen long rows of tables were set up, with benches on each side. It was very crowded and the gusting wind popped the sides of the tent in and out violently.

I paused, looking around. I was just about to suggest that we might be better off making a dash through the rain to eat in one of our vehicles, when Nathan pointed to an opening on a bench. I reluctantly caught up and stepped over the bench to sit down beside him.

"We best eat quickly," Nathan suggested. I followed his gaze to the far corner, where three men were repositioning a tent pole and fastening it to the ground.

I nodded in agreement and took a bite of the mashed potatoes. I felt the urge to raise my gaze and that's when I saw Joshua. He was sitting at the table across from us, and the Amish woman I'd met the night before was seated right next to him.

Our eyes met and I had to force the potatoes down with a hard swallow. Joshua's brows raised as his eyes shifted ever so slightly to look at Nathan. My heart pounded frantically and I worked to take a shallow breath. I had expected to see him, and thought I was prepared for the encounter, but all the bravado I'd felt the night before when Elayne had encouraged me to take the opportunity to make Joshua jealous had vanished. Now, in the light of day, I felt ashamed and silly. Seeing Joshua with his new girlfriend had upset me, not the other way around. I was so stupid.

I no longer heard the roaring wind or smelled the plate of food below my nose. Goosebumps rose on my arms, but I ignored the chilly air. The surprise that lit Joshua's face was quickly erased with the bland look of disinterest. His eyes clouded and his features hardened. Then he glanced away.

"CJ, are you all right?"

The wind and voices of dozens of people talking exploded in my head. I swiveled around. "What? What did you say?"

A troubled look flitted across Nathan's face. "You were a million miles away. I asked you if you had plans tomorrow."

I took a shaky breath. I wouldn't let Joshua bring me down. I had to move on and except the inevitable. Joshua Miller was not mine to pine over. He never was, and he never would be.

"I'm not really sure. If the weather clears, I might work on a painting." I tried to speak with enthusiasm, but feared I probably failed to sound convincing.

"There's a flea market in the next county over that you would enjoy. Local artists sell their work and there's even a country restaurant that has pretty good food." He motioned to his plate. "It doesn't hold a candle to this fare, but it's still good."

I was opening my mouth to agree to go, when I felt a soft touch on my arm. I looked down and it was Sylvia.

I turned to the child and patted my lap. She quickly perched herself on my legs, carefully placing her casted arm on the table.

"Are you feeling better today?" I asked the girl.

"Oh, yes. My arm doesn't hurt anymore. You're right. I am tough." She looked up at me proudly.

"Yes, you certainly are," I agreed.

"And who is this?" Nathan asked.

"This is Sylvia. She's my landlord's daughter."

Sylvia was reaching for my pie when she was suddenly lifted from my lap. I rounded to see a red-faced Joshua staring down at me. Without looking away, he spoke to his daughter with a low, yet irritated voice. I didn't need to understand the language to translate the mild scolding he gave the girl. Sylvia didn't look back as she left with her head downcast.

Anger swelled in my chest and I stood up, placing my hands on my hips. I was quite a bit shorter than Joshua, and hated having to crane my neck to look up at the man. "What was that all about?" I hissed. "She only wanted to say hello to me."

Joshua didn't speak. I saw the glint in his eyes, but he refused to open his mouth. It was his girlfriend who broke the tension-filled silence.

"I don't think we've officially met." She thrust her hand forward. "I'm Rosetta Bontrager. You're Joshua's tenant, aren't you?"

The woman's voice was all sweetness, but I wasn't fooled. She was claiming her position of authority over me, and her possession of Joshua. In that simple introduction, I realized just how formidable the Amish woman was. And she was pretty, too. Joshua took a step backward and stared off over the heads of the diners. I felt Nathan's eyes on me. I could only imagine what he was thinking. For a jolting second, I remembered being in the shed with Caleb Johnson, and how I had almost died. The world came back into focus and I forced my racing heart to slow.

I would not let Joshua turn me into a raving bitch. Life was too precious to fill it with drama I couldn't control. I was only in charge of my own behavior and how I reacted to things. I could be just as pleasant as any Amish woman could be.

I shook Rosetta's hand and forced cheerfulness. "I'm CJ." I gestured to Nathan. "This is my friend, Nathan. It's nice to meet you."

"I'd like to take a look in at the auction," Joshua told Rosetta. His eyes were only for her.

"Of course," she quickly replied. She turned once more to me. "I'm sure we'll see each other again, CJ."

I dropped back onto the bench when they had moved away. Finding my fork, I took a bite of the pie and chewed.

"That was little awkward," Nathan said slowly.

The corners of his mouth twitched, and I let out a bark of laughter. "You could say that."

We laughed together and it helped my shattered heart heal a little. Elayne was right. It was easier to deal with a breakup—even if the relationship wasn't real to begin with—when there was someone new at your side.

Whatever connection Joshua and I had once was clearly gone now. We both were moving on, and that was for the best.

Thunder rumbled overhead and the entire tent shook when a blast of wind struck it. I reached out and grabbed Nathan's arm. "I don't like being in this tent while it's storming. Do you mind if we finish our meal at my place?"

His face widened in surprise, and the happy look erased any doubts I had in my mind about inviting him.

"I think that's a great idea," he said in between glances at the shuddering canvas.

A short, red haired girl brought us a bag, and once we had gathered our food up, we rose from the table.

"CJ," a child's voice called out.

I lifted my head and searched the crowd. Nora was fast approaching. She held a cup, filled high with chocolate ice cream in her hands. I quickly searched the area for her father. Not seeing Joshua, my shoulders dropped and I waved at the girl.

The rolling boom that hit the tent deafened my ears. The canvas snapped up and the wooden poles groaned under the onslaught. Nathan reached for me and shouted. "We've got to get out of here!"

One moment, there were people talking and eating, and the next, panic shot through the crowd. A woman's scream was joined by the sound of men shouting.

Nathan's fingers dug into my shoulders. "Go, go!"

I twirled away from him and sprinted for Nora. Her smile had been replaced by a wide-eyed look of terror. Another blast of wind caught the tent, ripping the canvas from the poles. Dime-sized hail struck my head and a crash of flashing lightning blinded me for an instant. When I opened my eyes, I spotted Nora. She was frozen in fear. People ran past her, and when she was bumped, she fell to the ground.

Another gust of wind struck and I could barely stay on my feet—and then I heard an ear-splitting cracking noise.

The center pole had snapped.

Nora was beneath that wooden post. I stretched my legs and ran to her with all my strength.

Nora's hands reached out for me and I grabbed them, jumping sideways, and dragging her with me. She rolled against my side, and I wrapped my body protectively around her as the support came down.

There was an explosion in my head, and then I was swallowed in darkness.

12

JOSHUA

The cool wind smacking my face was a welcome sensation when I stepped outside of the tent. I picked Sylvia up, shielding her the best I could from the driving rain as I ran over the gravel road and into the auction barn. Rosetta had kept up with me and quickly went to wiping her face with a handkerchief she pulled from her pocket. She offered it to Sylvia, but the child tuned her face away, burying it in my wet shirt.

Rosetta ignored Sylvia's snub and tapped the child on the shoulder. "Come now. Let me wipe your face. It's all a mess."

Sylvia shook her head against my chest, not raising her eyes. Rosetta's face reddened considerably. She opened her mouth to say more, but I silenced her with a raised hand.

"It's all right. The child has experienced a lot of pain in the past couple of days. There's no need to push her about her face." I said it with as level a voice as I could manage. Seeing CJ with another man was bad enough, but when Sylvia climbed onto her lap, as if she were the woman's own child, I nearly lost it. I had overreacted, I know, but my emotions were still raw from my decision to stay away from the

English woman. I'd let myself slip by approaching CJ while I was full of jealousy and angst. Half the community had witnessed my behavior, and I was sure there were a lot of whispers flying around the tent after I left.

I swallowed and squeezed further inside the building, which was standing room only. The auctioneer was selling a cage with two doves in it. I coaxed Sylvia to look up at the birds when thunder boomed and the sky flashed white. A sickening crunch could be heard over the howling wind, and I turned back to the look at the tent.

A large portion of the canvas was flipped straight up, torn from the poles that had secured it. Men were gathering up their children and wives, and sprinting out into the rain. Sylvia was attached to me like a little crab, but I pried her away and handed her to Rosetta without words.

I raced back out into the storm, searching the chaos of those fleeing the giant tent that was breaking apart—but I was too late. I caught a glimpse of Nora's blue dress and her pale face, and then she was gone. The center pole, the largest of them all, tumbled down where my little girl had stood only seconds before.

"Nora!" I shouted into the wind. Hot tears stung my eyes as I climbed into the wreckage of what used to be a celebration tent.

The deluge let up slightly and the wind blew with less ferocity. I grabbed onto the downed canvas and tugged on it, praying to the Lord for more strength. I was joined by a throng of men. Loud calls for loved ones filled the damp air, but they sounded a million miles away.

"Were any of your children inside," a voice shouted into my ear. I looked up and saw Lester at my side.

"Nora was in the tent when it went down. Sylvia was with me." Icy panic gripped my heart when I thought of my son. "I don't know where John is."

"I'm here, Da!" John touched my back and our eyes met. His eyes were red rimmed and frightened. He had lost his mother and baby brother the previous year. The raw look of fear that he might lose a sister was evident on his face.

"No, no, it can't be…" I muttered through wet lips.

Lester grabbed my arm. "Stop!" he demanded. "Do you hear that?"

The low groan was coming from under the debris beneath us. I pulled my knife from my pocket and cut a long slit into the canvas. A hand reached out and I grasped it. Lester helped me pull the man through the opening I'd created.

The Englisher coughed and stumbled to his feet. It was the same man who CJ had introduced as her friend.

"Over here!" Nathan yelled, motioning us a few yards from where we'd just pulled him out.

Oh, my Lord. The tent collapsed on CJ, too.

I rushed to Nathan's side and grasped the heavy beam that held that part of the wreckage down. Lester was on my opposite side, and I heard the bishop shouting out orders to the other men to help us.

"On the count of three, men—all together. One, two, three!" I counted.

The beam, along with a large swath of heavy canvas, lifted in our hands. A strong woman knelt at my feet and latched onto the boots of a child. She pulled, quickly freeing a small boy.

"There's more trapped underneath!" Her voice was carried away on the wind, but I still heard her words.

The bishop's gaze locked with mine. "Come on, men. Everyone, heave! By the grace of God, we will cast this aside!"

The holy man's booming voice made the hair raise on the back of my neck. A shock wave of energy jolted my muscles and I strained even harder.

More men and women flooded in, until every inch of the length was covered.

"Lift!" Bishop Esch ordered.

The beam finally came loose and we shoved it aside. We'd uncovered several people. A man dropped alongside his wife, frantically talking to her. As I stumbled forward, I saw the woman open her eyes and begin responding to her husband. Another man carried a boy in his arms, and thankfully, the child was moving around and alert. Even the elderly woman, the last person freed from that section of tent, was sitting upright and rubbing her face as a younger woman held her hand.

My frozen gaze landed on the huge broken pole, lying on the ground. I couldn't breathe as I staggered over to it. The English man was close beside me, but I didn't glance his way. The word—*No*—pounded in my head, over and over again.

I reached the pole and leaned over it. There, only inches away, was CJ. She clutched my daughter in her arms.

Air finally filled my lungs. "Thank you, Jesus," I mumbled, swinging my legs over the pole to reach them.

I dropped into the mud and touched Nora's back. Her small body arched with gulping sobs, but when she looked over her shoulder, I knew she was physically all right. It was a miracle.

"Da," she sputtered, leaping into my arms.

I held her tightly to my chest. Her cap had come off and her long hair was a tangled mess down her back. I smoothed it the best I could, murmuring calming words into her ear.

I stared at CJ. I wanted to go to her, but Nathan was already helping her to her feet. She was muddy and wobbly, but otherwise, appeared to be in good condition.

Nora pulled back and sniffed, wiping the wetness from her eyes. "She saved me, Da. CJ saved me."

The rain turned to a sputtering drizzle and the clouds parted, revealing a shard of late afternoon sunshine. CJ finally looked up and our eyes locked. My chest tightened and my heart swelled.

"I know," I whispered to Nora. "I know she did."

13

CJ

"I hate to say it, CJ, but you really do have bad luck."

My gaze passed over Serenity. Her arms were crossed, and by the trembling of her lips, I could tell she was working hard not to smile.

"I'm glad you're entertained," I muttered, flinching when Beth, the EMT, pressed her cold fingers into my ribcage.

"Are they still tender?" she asked, dropping my shirt down.

"Sure, a little, but no worse than this morning, before the tent fell on me." I tried not to sound bitchy. After all, it was a miracle that Nora and I had survived, and that no one else in the community was seriously injured. "I don't need to go the hospital, do I?" Beth and Serenity exchanged glances and I felt a, *it's better to be safe than sorry* lecture coming, so I charged on. "Please, all I want to do is take a hot bath and rest in my own house tonight." I focused on Serenity's resistant face, which was now serious and contemplating. I added a twinge of pleading to my voice. "I spent weeks in that hospital. Don't make me go back there for observation when I feel perfectly fine."

"What do you think, Beth—can she safely go home?" Serenity asked the EMT.

My head swiveled to the older woman. Her short brown hair was streaked with gray. She was a no-nonsense kind of gal, and Beth knew all about how I was hospitalized after being attacked by the serial killer. She was one of the EMTs who had cared for me the night I had been rescued by Serenity.

I waited, holding my breath. Nathan stood a few feet away with his arms crossed over his chest. He hadn't left my side since the broken tent was pulled away. The sun had just set and there was a jarring contrast from the buttery light of dusk and the flashing ambulance and police cruiser lights. Serenity had been one of the first to arrive on the scene. With her usual high skill at multitasking, she quickly made her rounds, making sure no one was trapped or in dire straits. She still held a small notepad in her hands, but she'd paused from collecting information to pay special attention to my well-being. I glanced through the crowd and saw her fiancé, Daniel Bachman, talking to his parents and sister. His arm was around his mother's thin shoulders, and she was bent against him. It struck me that even though he had left the Amish, and had been shunned for doing so, he still had a relationship with his family.

"She can go home." I was about to climb out of the ambulance, when Beth raised her finger. "But I want you to see a doctor tomorrow—just stop in at the Urgent Care Center to get examined. If you feel dizzy or a bad headache comes on, please have someone take you to the emergency room, or call for an ambulance."

I slowly nodded. "I will, for sure. Thank you so much."

Serenity helped me step down onto the grass, even though I was perfectly capable of doing it myself. Her brow furrowed as she stared at me. "Are you really sure you're all right?"

The intense frown on her face nearly made me tear up. She was a good friend.

"I'm fine, really."

"I was just kidding earlier." Serenity's gaze shifted to the wreckage of the tent. "You're actually very lucky to be alive."

"I'm just glad no one else was seriously hurt," I said quietly.

"Do you need a ride home?" she asked.

Nathan stepped up. "I can take her home, Serenity. Or at the very least, follow her with my truck if she's up to driving."

Serenity gave Nathan a curt nod and settled her gaze on me again. "Are you okay with that?"

I tilted my head. She was the sheriff after all, and extremely paranoid.

"Yes, that works for me." I shooed Serenity away. "I'm okay, Serenity. You've got a lot on your plate here. You better go get to it."

Her gaze shifted between me and Nathan. "I'll call you later," she said. Then she disappeared into the throng of confused and shocked-looking people walking around.

Several horses had broken loose, and teenage boys were darting through the overturned buggies to catch them. A few strips of tin were peeled up on the schoolhouse, but the building was still standing, and that's all that really mattered.

I had heard the men talking about a down burst, or something like a mini tornado, that must have struck the tent. Now that everyone was safe and accounted for, there was chatter everywhere, from the smallest children to the elderly, speaking in rushed, excited voices. This certainly would give the community something to talk about for weeks to come.

"Are you ready to go home?" Nathan touched my arm and I didn't pull away.

My eyes scanned the schoolyard and the barn, where the auction had been held. There were too many bearded men, women in dresses, and children to count. I didn't see Joshua or his family, anywhere. A knot tightened my throat. He hadn't come to check on me, or even to say a few words of encouragement. He really didn't care at all.

The realization made me feel sick to my stomach. "Yes, let's go," I told Nathan.

When we arrived at my place, Nathan paused in the doorway. "Are you sure you don't need anything?" He was suddenly shy. "Maybe you would like some company for a little while?"

Nathan had done everything right. He'd been chivalrous and attentive throughout the storm, and its aftermath. I hated chasing him away after everything he'd done, but I really just wanted to be alone. I was still too upset about Joshua's behavior to give Nathan the attention he deserved. It wasn't fair to him. He was being so nice, and here I was, miserable and thinking about another guy.

"I appreciate the offer, and any other night, I'd take you up on it, but I'm exhausted. Please don't take it personally."

"I won't." He offered a small, more confident smile, and my heart melted a little. "Don't hesitate to call me for anything."

"I will, I promise. Thanks for"—I paused for the right words—"everything."

He chuckled. "Well, it wasn't exactly the first date I had hoped for, but it was definitely memorable."

Date? Yeah, I guess it was just that. "One for the books."

"We'll laugh about it someday." Nathan hesitated at the threshold. He suddenly leaned over and kissed my forehead. He was jogging down the porch steps before I had a chance to react. "I'll text you tomorrow," he said over his shoulder.

I frowned and automatically lifted my hand to wave. When I finally closed the door behind me, I slumped against it. Nathan was a great guy, and I didn't want to run him off, but there were no sparks between us. Not like with Joshua anyway.

"Joshua isn't available, and he doesn't want me anyway," I muttered to myself. I dropped my head back on the door and groaned. "I'm such a stupid fool."

14

JOSHUA

John caught Desperado's reins and headed back to the buggy. I breathed a sigh of relief that the horse hadn't acted up more. He had a fiery spirit and the storm had spooked him. Sylvia clung to my leg and Nora sat cross-legged in the grass, waiting. Rosetta was close by, talking to another woman in a hushed tone. She hadn't left my side since Nora and CJ had been rescued.

I glanced again at Rosetta. She was all businesslike, helping and instructing others. The other women flocked to her for leadership, and she was up to the task, but her clinginess for the past hour was getting on my last nerve. Again, I looked around to catch a glimpse of CJ—but she was nowhere to be found. When the sheriff had passed by, I was tempted to stop her and ask about her friend, and the woman who was tying my head in knots, but I had remained silent. Rosetta was close enough to hear if I inquired about CJ, and then there were others who would have noticed. I had been forced to show no interest in her well-being, even though she was strongly on my mind.

Bishop Esch had said that there were no serious injuries to report, and we had paused during cleanup to say a silent prayer, thanking

God for his protection in the storm. There was no reason to believe that CJ was in any kind of danger, but a quiet guilt racked my insides. I felt responsible for her, even though I had no reason to do so.

In a weak moment, I'd been tempted by CJ West. She was beautiful and sweet-natured, and smart to boot. It had been a mistake that I regretted, and couldn't take back. I'd asked the Lord for forgiveness, and I'd spoken directly to CJ about the impossibility of a relationship of any kind between us. I was trying very hard to do the right thing, but when the woman was nearby, all common sense went straight out the window. As much as I wanted to deny them, the feelings I had for CJ ran deep. I was beginning to think it was more than just an infatuation I had for her—and if that was really the case, what could I ever do about it?

I closed my eyes and rubbed them, trying to wipe CJ West from my mind.

"How did your family fare?" Aaron asked. His voice startled me and I blinked at him before answering.

"All are well and accounted for." I lifted my chin to the schoolhouse. "Nana is handing out bandages and John is fetching our horse."

"By the grace of God, it wasn't far worse." The bishop smoothed down his beard and raised bushy white eyebrows at me. "There was a guardian angel among us, I hear."

His gaze strayed to Nora, who was picking blades of grass and tossing them aside.

I swallowed. "Sure enough, there was. My tenant pulled Nora out of the way of the pole crashing down. If she hadn't been so brave, my daughter wouldn't be sitting over there right now."

The bishop's lips pursed and he looked like his mind was busy. The silence was heavy, but I didn't have the heart to speak for the sake of it. I couldn't stop Aaron from his own ideas about the situation with CJ. He was a very perceptive man.

"CJ is a fine woman for an Englisher. But you would never be truly happy with her because she would never be content with your lifestyle and beliefs." I began to interrupt him and he silenced me with a thrust of his hand and a hasty voice. "I am no fool, Joshua. I see the way you look at that woman. The best thing that could happen is that she leaves your cottage and our community for good. You'll get no peace as long as she's close by."

My heart pounded and my mind shot in several directions at once. "Have you reconsidered your decision?"

The bishop made a *tsk tsk* sound. "Not precisely. It is on my mind, though. The ministers and I can make your life easier by eliminating your temptation, but will that create a solid man in our community—one who would be a good match for my niece? I think not. You must face your demons, Joshua, or they'll always haunt you."

"You misunderstand. CJ has been through a lot and I feel some responsibility for her. I don't want to hurt her after everything she's been through. There's nothing more going on between us." I had spoken with as much conviction as I could muster, but the bishop's face remained rigid.

"Do you see my gray hair and beard?" Aaron asked, and of course I nodded. "I have been around long enough to become quite good at reading people." He leaned in. "That girl has a fondness for you, as well. Please don't take my calm handling of this situation as any kind of acceptance or approval of it. I am simply trying to save you from a lot of grief—and my niece has shown favor toward you. She's a special young woman, and one who wouldn't be content with just any man. I feel the two of you would make a good match. I will do what I can to facilitate that joining, but mark my words, Joshua. I will not stand by and witness your destruction of her heart and spirit. You must decide the future you want for you...and for your children. Lest you forget that your actions will affect them greatly."

"I understand. You have nothing to worry about," I tried to convince him, as much as myself.

"I hope not." The bishop left suddenly, and for a moment I was alone. Sylvia had sat down beside her sister, and John was finishing up the last of the harness straps. Rosetta moved away when her uncle had appeared, and now she assisted two other women in picking up the trash that had blown across the parking area.

The bishop's words were unnerving, but they rang true. If I didn't somehow get CJ out of my head, I might make a mistake that could not be undone. One that would hurt Nana and my children. But the seedling of a thought pestered me, and I decided that it wouldn't be fair to either of us if I didn't at least consider the possibility of a compromise when it came to the English woman.

15

CJ

I slunk down lower in the water until just my head was above the bubbly surface. It was almost too hot, but I enjoyed the cooking sensation that loosened my muscles and caressed my skin. Steam had fogged up the tiny window near the ceiling, but I could still see the outline of the inky darkness outside. The candles burning provided the only light in the bathroom. For a few short hours the electricity had spontaneously begun to work again. It was just enough time to heat the water, and get the bath drawn, but within seconds of climbing in, the lights flickered and went out again. I'd grabbed my robe and streaked into the kitchen to gather the candles. I wasn't going to let the lack of electricity ruin my bath.

I took a sip of red wine and returned the glass to the ledge of the tub, before exhaling. I wished I hadn't chased Nathan off. There was a good chance he would have known how to fix the electricity. It was too late to do anything about it at this late hour. I'd call an electrician in the morning and be done with it. I certainly wouldn't bother Joshua with it again. Taking care of it myself and sending him the bill was the most sensible thing to do.

I was proud of myself for being so pragmatic. I certainly wasn't helpless, and if I was going to stay here for the time being, I would have to step up and do more maintenance. Because I certainly wasn't calling Joshua.

I blew out a hard breath, spraying bubbles everywhere. It wasn't going to be easy, living here for even a few more days, but it would take at least that long to find another place to rent. Yes, my mind was made up. I couldn't stay in the Amish cottage any longer than absolutely necessary. Being around Joshua and watching him with his new girlfriend would drive me crazy. I wasn't that good. Some things were just too difficult to deal with, and Joshua Miller was one of those things.

Ideas swirled in my head. Perhaps I could find another house to rent in the country—one not owned by an Amish man? I'd probably have to move out of the area to locate the right place, though, and I'd just gotten used to living in Blood Rock. I would miss Serenity, too. She had mentioned an apartment available in town, but was living directly in a small town what I was looking for? Probably not. The entire reason I came here was to create folksy art, and I was doubtful whether I could manage it if I didn't have the barns, chickens, cows, fields, and horses to draw inspiration from. I know I could always just drive to such places, but I gathered more of a muse from living right in the middle of it.

I swished the water around with my hand as a thought occurred to me. I could take a bunch of photographs tomorrow morning, and create art using them. I grinned in the dark. It was a good idea, and one that might just work.

"CJ! Are you all right?"

I froze in the water. Why was Joshua in my house, calling out to me?

I didn't get the chance to answer him when the door flew open and he strode in.

I submerged even further under the water. Thank God for the bubbles and flickering candlelight.

"What are you doing in here—are you nuts?" I shouted. "Get out!"

Joshua turned off the flashlight he was waving around and grabbed the hat off his head as he backed away. "I'm sorry, CJ. I thought something was wrong when I saw the lights out and you didn't answer the door." He bumped into the wall and mumbled a curse, before ducking out the door.

"What the heck! I was just taking a bath. I can't hear knocking on the door from here. Who stops by for a spontaneous visit at"—I glanced at my phone as I stood up and jerked the robe off the hook—"eight-thirty at night?"

I wrapped the plush material around me and tied the strap with a hard tug. The candles didn't provide enough light for me to properly see my reflection in the mirror. But I still took a second to scrunch my wet curls and pinch my cheeks, although I guessed I was already deeply flushed.

Hot blood coursed through my veins and my heart felt like a bobbing balloon. *What was the stupid man thinking?*

I paused to listen and the house was quiet. The thought that Joshua might have rudely barged in on my bath, and then just left, wasn't far from my mind when I strode into the kitchen.

Just enough moonlight sprayed in the windows to illuminate his outline. He sat at the table, with his hands clasped in front of him.

Before I could say anything, he spoke up. His voice shook. "I'm truly sorry. It didn't occur to me you were bathing in the dark."

"It wasn't completely dark," I snapped. "I had candles. Don't you remember about the electricity not working properly?"

"I saw the lights on this morning when I passed by. They worked at that time." His voice had regained its usual condescending tone and I flinched.

"It came back on this morning, making me think the electric company had some kind of issue, and maybe it wasn't the house at all. Either way, there's still a problem that needs to be taken care of." I worked hard to keep my voice restrained.

"I'll call them first thing in the morning. I should have taken care of it today, but with the benefit dinner and Sylvia's arm, I was just too distracted to get it done. I'm sorry about that."

I suddenly felt silly for being so upset. Joshua must have been concerned about me to go racing around the house like a crazy man—and after everything that had happened today, it was understandable.

I drew in a long breath. "How is Sylvia feeling? And Nora—is she okay?"

He nodded. "They're both fine. At first, Sylvia wouldn't stop crying. She saw the tent go down and it scared her something awful." He licked his lips. "Nora is her usual self, being stubbornly silent about the entire thing. They both fell asleep in the buggy on the way home. They're snug in their beds, and even John turned in early."

"How about Nana?"

I caught the lift of his mouth in the semi-darkness. "She's fine as well." He chuckled a little. "She warned the bishop and the other ministers to cancel the event when the forecast turned ugly, and you know what? She chose to eat her meal in the kitchen, instead of the tent."

"Smart woman," I commented, leaning back against the refrigerator.

Neither one of us spoke for a moment. I could almost stroke the friction in the air between us. I was acutely aware of the water droplets streaming between my breasts, and my nakedness beneath the robe.

The silence and Joshua's staring eyes became unbearable. "Well, as you can see"—I spread my arms wide—"I'm perfectly fine. You can get back to your family—and your girlfriend."

He smacked the air with his raised hands. "Whoa. Rosetta is not my girlfriend."

"Then what is she?" I hated myself for even asking.

He fidgeted with his fingers on the tabletop and glanced away. When his eyes returned, he looked guarded. "She is a widow who is visiting this community. There are some in the community wishing to match us up." He tilted his head and his blue-eyed gaze bore into me, causing my heart to skip. "I am not interested in such a union at this time."

I raised my brows. Fiery energy stirred my emotions. "I bet that one of them is the bishop, right?"

He nodded once.

"What are you waiting for? Rosetta's pretty and available. She's also Amish—the perfect match." I tried, but couldn't keep the sulkiness from my voice.

Joshua's eyes widened and he took a large breath, then exhaled slowly. His gaze drifted over me, pausing for a few heartbeats on my chest, where my robe had slipped a little. I quickly drew in the material and folded my arms tightly.

I lifted my chin. "Well? Don't you have anything to say?"

In a sudden movement, he was out of the chair and across the small room. He stopped just inches away from me.

"Why are you making this so difficult? I am trying to be an honorable man—for you and me. I never meant to hurt you—God knows that."

I shook my head. My gaze dropped to the floor, stopping on my bare feet next to Joshua's booted ones. I couldn't have this conversation with him while I was in a robe. My heart raced and my belly trembled—and not from fear or discomfort. My insides ached with anticipation. I fought my body with everything I had not to lean into Joshua and press my breasts to his chest. I wanted desperately to slip my hands up his wide shoulders and down his muscled arms. My veins pulsed for this man I could never have.

I bit my bottom lip and closed my eyes. "Can't you just leave me alone?" I begged in a harsh whisper.

Joshua moved closer and I felt his warm breath on my face. Startled, my eyes popped open. He was only inches away, with his hands bracing the refrigerator on each side of me. I was essentially trapped between his strong arms. I wanted to be angry, but my stomach betrayed me, like a million butterflies taking flight. I had dreamed of Joshua Miller's hard body pressed against me for months, and now that it was actually happening, I froze. My mind screamed, *no, don't be foolish*! But, oh, how every other part of me screamed to kiss him.

"CJ…" his voice was clipped with restraint, but his eyes were pools of passion.

I swayed a little and Joshua's mouth met mine. He kissed me softly, sweetly, at first, but I was impatient and my blood was on fire. The kiss deepened as I slid my tongue along his. He groaned into my mouth, and I sighed with a hunger I'd never felt before. Kissing Joshua was the most natural thing in the world.

How could anything that felt so right be so wrong?

Joshua's hand cupped my face and he said my name again. He trailed kisses across my cheek, and then along my jaw until he found my neck. My legs became jelly, but his other hand gipped my hip, holding me steady. I shifted my leg, bending my knee against his side, and he lifted me up, pressing me back against the refrigerator. I wrapped my legs around his waist. I needed to be even closer to him.

When his hand finally slipped inside the robe, finding my breast, I moaned into his ear. He mumbled something unintelligible, and then his lips were back on mine.

Clip, clop, clip, clop.

The sound of hoof beats on pavement reached my ears. Joshua

stiffened, leaning back to listen. He took a raspy breath and the beating of his heart against my palm was pounding. We held our breaths as the rhythmic sound came close, and then fell off, drifting farther away.

My groin still tingled and the hammering of my heart matched Joshua's, but the moment was gone. I lowered my legs and wiggled out of his embrace. A low growl escaped his lips, but he let me go. When I tried to turn and back even further away from him, his hand snatched my wrist.

"CJ, don't…"

I snorted. "We're like a couple of ninth graders, sneaking around and trying to make out without getting caught." I rubbed my forehead in frustration. "It's ridiculous."

"We can't be together. You know that." He spoke softly, but the words boomed in my head.

"What the hell are you doing? Huh?" I knew my eyes were wild. I pulled back and stared at him with parted lips. "I'm not the one who walked in on you taking a bath, Joshua."

"I was worried about you—" he offered, but I interrupted him.

"About my safety, or were you afraid that Nathan might be here with me?" I spat.

His eyes narrowed. "Has your relationship progressed that far?"

My mouth dropped open. "Of course not," I huffed.

"You think you have the right to accuse me of courting Rosetta, when you have already moved on with an Englishman."

"He is just a friend."

"Just like Rosetta is my friend."

I stood frozen, not able to glance away. He scrunched his lips and I knew he wanted to lean in and kiss me again. His desire was as strong as my own—but it didn't matter. It was impossible, and I wasn't going to make the same mistake again.

"I'm leaving, Joshua. Just as soon as I can get someplace else lined up, I'm out of here. We won't be able to keep our hands off each other. Tonight proves that."

His face became stony, and his jaw twitched. "There is another way."

I wrapped the robe around me and tilted my head. "What are you talking about?"

He swallowed, hesitated, and then became resolved. "You could become Amish."

16

JOSHUA

"Are you serious?" CJ looked back at me with wide-eyed shock.

I pushed my hat up. The reckless suggestion came from my heart. I didn't see any other way we could be together. The idea had been a whisper in my mind since we'd gone horseback riding. CJ was right. It wasn't possible to continue on the course we were. As long as she was close by, I wouldn't be able to get her out of my head. Even if she left, I'd still wallow in the memories of the feel of her soft skin and the warm, spicy scent of her curly hair. As it was now, I saw her bright green eyes whenever I closed my own. Somehow, I'd fallen in love with the English woman. I wouldn't let her go without at least making the offer. But now, after seeing her reaction, I felt like a fool. She didn't have the same deep feelings I had for her, and she'd never leave her comfortable life, full of conveniences and modern technology to be with me.

"It's just a possibility, something for you to think about."

"Why don't you stop being Amish?" she asked, crossing her arms under her breasts.

I was expecting the question, but it still left me at a loss for words. I walked across the kitchen, and back again. The moon had risen higher in the night sky beyond the window, and it provided enough light that I clearly saw CJ's pouting mouth. Enough with talking. I wanted to sweep her up in my arms, but her rigid stance made me keep my distance.

I let out a heavy sigh. "I cannot leave my way of life, CJ. If I did, it would mean forcing my children to do so as well—and that's not right. They must make that decision for themselves one day. I will not choose their paths for them."

"Would it be so bad for them to go English? They'd be able to attend school through twelfth grade, and drive cars. They could wear normal clothes, and go to the movies with friends—and then there's college and a career of their choice. They'd have so many more opportunities." Her tone was a mixture of eagerness and pleading.

My heart turned to stone and I shook my head. "Are those things so very important to you? My children will grow up playing ball games and riding their horses. They will make lifelong friends, who will always be there for them. When they finish school, John will have time to focus on learning a trade of his choice, and the girls will be taught by Nana and the other women in the community, all the things they'll need to know to make fine wives for good husbands. They'll be just as happy as any Englisher—and they won't be corrupted by the evil in the outside world. My children will grow up with true faith in God and His teachings. That is something I doubt they'd get in your world." As I talked, CJ's brow furrowed and her mouth pursed. Only minutes earlier, I'd kissed those pouty lips, and now, anger stirred our insides. "I have seen many Englishers who don't seem very happy, and I have even wondered how content you are with your own life." She took a sharp breath and I plowed on. I wanted to hurt her, like she was hurting me. "We are too different, you and I. It was a mistake for me

KAREN ANN HOPKINS

to even suggest such a thing as you leaving your comfortable life to be with me and my children."

She took a step forward and jabbed her finger into my chest. Her robe gaped, revealing the smooth white swell of her breasts. I quickly looked away.

"The mistake was for you to assume that it was all right to ask me to give up my life, but you weren't willing to even consider doing the same thing yourself." I dared to glance back. Her wild curls bounced around her head with her movements, and her eyes flashed. She took a breath and when she spoke again, her voice was strung tight. "I get it, Joshua, I really do. You have kids, and they have to be your priority. I also understand that you like farming, and the comradery you have with your people. I admit, I kind of envy that part of being Amish— but there's problems everywhere—even in this community."

CJ's words became impassioned. "I would be happy to live on a farm with a hard-working man like you. I love your kids and Nana. The horses are wonderful, and the view is breathtaking. I know I could make friends and I certainly don't mind cleaning house and cooking meals—as long as I still had time to paint." Her face saddened and my chest clenched. "I would be happy, except for the part of losing my freedom. I believe every individual has the right to make their own decisions. I couldn't stand having a handful of men telling me how to live my life. That's why I couldn't convert to being Amish. It's not your way of life that bothers me, it's the rules you have to live by."

Her words settled over me like a wet blanket and I slumped, feeling exhausted and hollow. CJ was a wise woman. Her beauty had initially caught my attention, but it was her mind, and her spunky nature that captured my heart. A love affair between the two of us was impossible. I understood that, but the emptiness that gripped me told me that walking away from CJ West would be the hardest thing I ever had to do—besides burying my wife and little son. CJ had somehow lifted the dark cloak I'd been living under for so long. She was sunshine and warmth, where my life had been cold and unbending. I didn't want to let her go—but I had to—before the passion I felt for her made me do something I'd regret later.

"You're welcome to stay on as long as you need to, but it probably is best that you move on with your life elsewhere. I fear that neither one of us is strong enough to fend off the constant temptation we'll have in each other's company." Our eyes locked, and I saw disappointment in those lovely green depths.

CJ was too proud to show me her hurt. She raised her chin and nodded. "Yeah, you're right. No need to put off the inevitable. I'll start looking around"—she paused, sucking in a deep breath—"for somewhere to go."

I began to take a step toward her but stopped and turned on my heel. I went through the screen door without looking back. The walk up the driveway was the longest of my life, as I dragged my feet over the gravel. The breeze was stiff enough to unsettle the leaves. They fluttered down from the maple trees, skipping across the driveway.

I stared up at the starry night sky and implored, "Why, God? Why have you brought this pain into my life? Are you testing my strength?" I grunted. "Lord, you know my limits, but losing CJ is breaking me in two. It's so unfair that for the first time since my wife and baby boy died, I've found someone who makes me feel alive, and now she's being snatched away."

I bent my head. Somehow, I would have to carry on for the children's sake, if for no other reason.

17

CJ

I sipped my coffee and rocked in the chair on the front porch, surveying the spectacular view of the farm. My focus turned to the white house on top of the hill. I had heard the hoof beats while I was still in bed. I'd tossed and turned for hours before finally falling into an exhausted sleep sometime in the early hours of the morning. The *clip clops* had woken me. I wondered where Joshua was off to at such an early hour. Perhaps to help with the cleanup of the schoolyard after the storm? Or maybe he was visiting Rosetta.

Either way, I shouldn't care. Our relationship had been decided the night before. For all the hot passion between us, we could never be together. I had pretty much resolved myself to that surety weeks ago, but after the horseback ride and the heavy make out session, I'd experienced a surge of hope that we had a chance. I was even humbled that Joshua would mention the possibility of me becoming Amish. His feelings must run deep to even say such a thing.

I paused my rocking to search out Gypsy in the grassy field. At that very moment, she raised her head and nickered in my direction. I held my breath. It was as if the horse knew that I was looking for her, and she basically said, *here I am*! For a second, I had even enter-tained the idea of making a go of being Amish. I had never felt so drawn to man as I did Joshua. When he actually let his guard down, like on our trail ride, he was fun to talk to. I loved his old-fashioned politeness, and especially the way he sometimes seemed reserved, and other times, he was as fierce as a lion. The attraction between us could not be denied. I'd grown close to his children and Nana, and I didn't want to leave Gypsy and this beautiful farm. Were all those things worth throwing away my freedom? I'd never be able to drive a car or even wear a pair of jeans again. I wanted to slap my shallow mind for thinking about such trivial things, but deep down, I knew those two grievances were just the tip of the iceberg of changes I'd have to accept in my life if I went Amish.

I finished the coffee off with a gulp. No, even if I truly loved Joshua, and I wasn't convinced that I did, I would come to resent everything I had to give up to be with him. The fact that he didn't want me enough to leave his life behind, sealed the deal. I needed to go inside and make some phone calls. Serenity would point me in the right direction for a new place to rent. Maybe even Elayne would have some ideas. Going back to Indy wasn't an option at the moment. I hadn't accomplished my goals just yet. If nothing else came from my stay in the quaint countryside, I would at least create the paintings I'd always dreamed about. I wasn't going to allow a broken relationship, or whatever you wanted to call it, to stop me from getting the job done. When I had a collection, I'd take them back to the city, contact some old friends in the art community, and set up a show. I already had several paintings completed. I just needed a few more.

Sluggishly, I rose. For all my inner pep talking, I felt empty in-side. The only way to avoid heartbreak was to remain forever single—which was now my plan.

"CJ!"

I turned and saw Nana walking quickly down the driveway in my direction. For an ancient woman, she was still quite spry, but I jogged down the porch steps to shorten her journey.

"Hello, Nana. Are you feeling all right?" I shielded my eyes from the sunshine as she stopped in front of me with a loud grunt.

"As well as can be expected at my age." She flashed a toothy smile. "I am in need of a favor, though. I promised Katherine I'd stop by her house to help her with her laundry. She hurt her arm yesterday, pulling one of her little ones out of debris."

I brought my hand to my mouth. Katherine was one of the Amish women who had been kind to me when I'd first moved in.

"They had fled the tent into the schoolhouse before it went down, but one of her children fell behind, and a portion of the torn canvas knocked the boy down, covering him. He's a tough lad, and is fine, but Katherine wrenched her arm pretty well as she freed him." She caught her breath. "I had a driver lined up, but she called a few minutes ago, saying she was sick and couldn't take me."

I glanced up and watched Nora and Sylvia hanging laundry on the clothes line, which hooked from the porch to a pole halfway across the yard. "What about the kids?"

"John is here to watch them. I shouldn't be too long helping Katherine." Nana looked impatient and I grinned. When she wanted to do something, there was no stopping her.

"Of course. I'd be happy to drive you over there. I'll just grab my purse and car keys."

Before I turned, Nana stopped me. "I didn't have the opportunity to thank you for saving our dear Nora. Everyone is talking about how you risked your own life to grab the child out of harm's way. I will forever be in your debt, my girl."

Tears pooled in my eyes and I quickly wiped them with my fingertips, sniffing. "It was nothing. I'm just happy she didn't get hurt."

"At the very least, I owe you a home cooked meal," Nana said firmly.

I wondered what Joshua would think of Nana's offer, but dismissed the worry. I would be gone soon enough. I might as well enjoy Nana's company until then.

"It's a deal," I said.

Katherine hurried up to the car door. Her creamy complexion was like porcelain, and the white cap and maroon dress made her look even more like a doll. "I applaud your bravery yesterday, CJ. You prevented certain tragedy by your quick action."

My skin heated uncomfortably. "Thanks for saying that, but I didn't give it much thought. I sort of just reacted."

She smiled with genuine warmth. "You are too modest. Please come in and have some tea with me. With my daughter and Nana working on the laundry together, the job should be finished in no time at all."

Part of me really wanted to make up an excuse, any little white lie I could come up with to politely decline the invitation. But the other part was intrigued with the idea of spending some time with the Amish woman. I couldn't shake my morbid fascination with the lifestyle, even though I knew it wasn't for me.

When I nodded that I would join Katherine, her face brightened and she opened the car door for me. We walked through the yard together. Tentacles of wood smoke drifted on the breeze from the chimney, and I breathed in the hickory scent. It was nice. The sunshine was deceiving. There was a crispness in the air that made me zip up my sweater jacket.

I followed Katherine past a pile of shiny orange pumpkins and down a few steps to the basement door. She looked over her shoulder. "I have instructions for my daughter before we retreat upstairs. Cynthia tries hard, but she's a bit rough with our old ringer washer. I'm afraid if she isn't careful, she'll break it again."

I smiled and nodded, like I understood what she was talking about, but I was actually clueless. A loud vibrating noise shook my eardrums when we entered the basement. The huge area had a cement floor that was immaculately swept. In one corner was a box freezer, counter, and a line of cupboards. The rest of the walls were vacant, except for a broom and a few black coats hanging on pegs, and some shelves filled with colorful jars of canned goods.

Nana was already working beside a young girl, who I guessed to be around twelve or thirteen. They hovered over a strange looking contraption above a tub. There was another basin right beside it.

Katherine shouted orders to her daughter in their language. The front of the girl's dress was soaking wet, and I soon understood why. Nana's hands were submerged in sudsy water. I caught the scent of bleach and wrinkled my nose, wondering how she could submerge her bare hands in the harsh water. I watched her work with the material, a white button up shirt, in the wash water before she dropped it into the rinse water. Very quickly, she swirled the shirt around, and then balled it up, squeezing some of the water out with her gnarly hands. Then she passed the garment over to Cynthia, who began to feed it though the strange looking contraption. Katherine said something and the girl slowed her pulling movements. A moment later, she had freed the shirt from the ringer, but even so, it was still a lot wetter than clothes coming out of regular washing machine, following the spin cycle. She dropped the dripping wet material into an already full basket of similarly wet clothes. Bending her knees, she hoisted the basket up onto her tiny hip, grunted, and headed for the side door. As I listened to Katherine and Nana talking, I couldn't understand what they were saying, and even if I did speak the language, the sound of the motor drilled into my head. I caught up with Cynthia and took hold of the one side of the basket.

She paused. "Are you going to help me?"

"Sure. It looks like you need it," I said.

The basket was heavy, even with us sharing the weight, and water dripped out of it in a stream that splashed my leg and foot. Now I understood why the poor girl was so wet.

We stopped beneath the clothes line and I followed Cynthia's lead, hanging the shirts upside down, with two wooden pins. With us working silently together, we got the clothes hung quickly.

"CJ! Come to the house!" Katherine called out from an upstairs window.

I glanced at Cynthia. "Sorry…"

She laughed. "You're soaked, like me." She clutched the edges of her blue dress and spread it wide.

I chuckled, but the cool breeze made me shiver. "Do you do the laundry the same way in the wintertime?"

"Ya. It's always the same." She nudged my arm with her elbow. "That's why I work fast. Thank you for joining the party." She winked and I saw mischief in her eyes. Would the spunky Cynthia be like Elayne or Daniel, and leave the community for adventures in the outside world? Only time would tell.

I patted the girl's back and then jogged over to the house. When I entered the front door, a blast of heat hit me from the wood burning stove. The aroma of baking sugar assailed my nose.

"Do you like oatmeal cookies?" Katherine hurried to meet me with a cup of tea.

I took the mug and sat down at the table. There were two toddlers sitting on the floor with a pile of wooden blocks between them. "How many children do you have?" I asked.

She pulled the tray of cookies from the oven and set it on the counter. "Only six now. I lost my eldest son in an accident last year." She sounded sad.

I recalled Elayne's story about Eli Bender, and felt bad for asking. "I'm sorry."

"Eli is with our Lord. He's in a much better place than the rest of us." She used the spatula to transfer the cookies to a plate, and deposited it in front of me. When she took the seat across from me, she crossed her arms on the table and looked at me with what I can only describe as hawkish curiosity.

"How are you feeling, CJ? Is your body healed from"—she paused, searching for words—"what happened to you during the summer?"

"I'm feeling much better, thank you."

"And your mind?" She nudged the dish closer to me. "It can be difficult to recover from trauma. I know. When my son was taken from me." She shuddered. "I wasn't myself for a long time."

I took a cookie and bit into it, and it melted in my mouth. To say it was delicious was an understatement. "This tastes amazing." I sighed after another bite, and then I swallowed. "I've been seeing a therapist. She's helped me a lot."

"I see," she said quietly. "Joseph told me the bishop and ministers have allowed you to stay Joshua's. How is that going?"

Her tone was friendly, but very intense. I sat up straighter. "I really appreciate the elders bending the rules for me, but I've decided to move on from the cottage on the Miller's farm."

Her eyes widened. "I don't understand. I thought you liked it there."

"I do…but, it's complicated." I glanced out the window, hoping my face didn't give anything away.

She leaned in. "The Lord is constantly challenging us. It's strange how oftentimes, when we finally get what we want, we change our minds." I met her melancholy gaze. "Perhaps it's for the best. Even though we'll miss you when you leave, you'll have more opportunities to meet people living on the outside." The corner of her mouth lifted. "I saw you with a gentleman friend at the benefit dinner. Has he helped you make the decision?"

I suddenly realized that Katherine wasn't just curious, she was gossipy. The inside of the house was warm, and hearing the children's soft murmurs, made me a little sleepy. I covered a yawn with my hand. If I didn't have TV or internet, or get to drive my car, I'd probably be more interested in my neighbor's love life, too. "Nathan is a nice guy, and a friend, but that's about it."

"For now, anyway. Time has a way of changing the heart."

She said it in a teasing tone, but I still bristled. "Sometimes not for the best."

The front door flung open and a boy ran in. I guessed his age to be around eight-years-old, and he was out of breath. He shot me a surprised look and then rattled something off to his mom in their language. Her face dropped and she shook her head. "All right, then. Thanks for taking the call, Marlan. Best go tell your father."

The boy spun on his heels and was gone. Before he closed the door, a quick blast of biting wind perked me up. Katherine's face was tight with agitation. "Is everything okay?" I feared the worst.

"A bug must be going around the drivers." She snorted softly. "Ours just called. He isn't feeling well, and had to cancel our trip."

"Where were you going?" I asked to be conversational.

"Just a trip to Ohio for my cousin's wedding. Jeffry was supposed to pick us up this afternoon, and return us home tomorrow." Her eyes brightened and then narrowed slightly as she looked at me. "I see you drove Nana here. Are you interested in another job?"

"Job?" I couldn't stop the bubble of laughter from leaving my mouth. "It was hardly that. I was just doing Nana a favor so she could help you out with the laundry." Her doll-like face deflated and I felt bad for her. "Are you close to your cousin?"

She shrugged. "I have over two dozen cousins, and Rachel and I are close, but honestly"—she glanced around and lowered her voice—"it would be so nice to get away. My sister, who's heavy in pregnancy, wasn't going, so she offered to keep my children. It's the first time since Joseph and I were married eighteen years ago that we were taking a night away without any of the children."

I sucked in a breath. "Eighteen years without a night off from the kids?"

She nodded. The smile on her face was forced and sad. "With so many more important things happening in the community, I'm a selfish woman for even daring to complain about the loss of one silly night alone with my husband." She sighed. "There will be other opportunities, I'm sure."

I shook my head. "No, you're not going to miss your special date night."

"But how? Several drivers are sick, and it's too late to make other arrangements—"

"Because I'm going to take you, Katherine. I might not be an Amish driver, but after going eighteen years with seven kids and no time away with your husband, I think you're long overdue for this trip."

She jumped from her chair and hurried around the table. The tight hug startled me.

"Oh, thank you! Thank you! You really are an angel, CJ West."

18

JOSHUA

I glanced out the window at the cars zooming by. The van was crowded and my legs were cramped, but I was still grateful for the opportunity to get away from Blood Rock for a night. When Lester had turned his buggy into the driveway that morning, I hadn't been expecting an invitation to catch a ride with him to my nephew's wedding in Ohio. With tensions rising between me and CJ, and the fact that I hadn't slept a wink the night before, I was more than ready to do something—anything—to keep my mind off of my longings for a woman I couldn't have. Nana, sensing my gloomy state, offered to care for the children overnight so that I could go.

I closed my eyes and forced the buzz of quiet conversation around me to disappear. CJ was once again in my arms. She fit perfectly against me. Her body was soft and willing. I remembered the curve of her hips and the fullness of her breasts. Her scent was intoxicating. I blew out a deep breath. We had been so close to losing ourselves in that embrace.

"Will you be staying with the Masts?"

My eyes popped open, and Lester's face came into focus. Beside him was his wife, Esther. Every seat was full. Traveling to weddings was a main priority for most of my people, and Blood Rock was no different.

"Yes. I talked to my sister briefly, and she said she has a couple of cabins at the back of her property that I have the pick of," I replied, rubbing my chin. I was glad for the distraction Lester's talkative ways afforded me.

"I stayed in one of those cabins a few years ago, when I went to the Maple Ridge community to deer hunt with my cousins. Your brother-in-law is a very generous man. I've heard he loans the cabins out to anyone in his community who has visitors in need of a place to stay," Lester said.

"He is that. I'm looking forward to seeing him and my sister. It's been a few years."

We had exited the highway, and I turned my attention to the orange and yellow landscape beyond the window. The land was flat here, so different from the rolling hills of my new Indiana community. The movement of the van and the lack of sleep from the previous night began to affect me. I closed my eyes and welcomed the sleep.

I crossed my arms on the railing and leaned over. The Mast boys were having a little competition with their Belgians. The two teams of giant, cream colored horses were a sight to behold. Their harnesses shined in the waning light and their muscles strained as their hooves dug into the dirt.

"Come on, David!" One of the men on the railing shouted.

It looked like most of the community had turned out to see the brothers compete at pulling the loads of logs across the field. Whichever team of horses crossed the finish line first won nothing more than bragging rights, but for a man who farmed with his horses, that was reward enough. The race was also one of the community's activities before the big wedding in the morning. A smile toyed at the corner my mouth. When I had married Miranda, there had been a horse race the night before as well. Only that one was a mounted speed competition, and I had won. I finished several lengths in front of the nearest challenger.

"They're fine horses."

I looked over my shoulder. It was Rosetta. I wasn't surprised that she was there. Most of Blood Rock's inhabitants knew the families of either the bride, groom, or both, and had traveled to Ohio for the wedding.

"Are you a horsewoman?" I asked.

Rosetta pressed against the railing, watching the horses pull their loads. "When I was girl, I rode every day. I still fancy them, but seldom do I get the opportunity to really enjoy them."

An image of CJ leisurely grooming Gypsy with a huge smile plastered on her full lips, filled my mind. I gave my head a small shake and tried to focus on the woman beside me—a perfectly good woman, who seemed to enjoy my company.

"Horses have always been a passion of mine. These Belgians are some of the finest I've seen in a while." We lapsed into comfortable silence. There were the sounds of spectators calling out encouragement to the young men, and the smell of grilling hamburgers on the cool breeze. "Are you here for the bride or groom?" I asked politely.

"Neither." She glanced sideways. "I have no close relations here— that I know of. My uncle convinced me it would be fun. I caught a ride over with the Yoders."

Following Aaron's little speech after the tent collapsed, he'd probably feared I wasn't in the right frame of mind for his niece. Therefore, he'd come up with a diversion for Rosetta, sending her off to another community for a couple of days to see how she liked it. I hardly blamed him. I hadn't shown as much interest in the woman as I should have. Since I was here for pretty much the same reason as Rosetta—seeking a distraction from a difficult situation—it seemed prophetic that we'd bump into each other.

"I hear there will be over five hundred in attendance tomorrow." There was so much tension whenever I was around CJ. The attraction I felt for the English woman made it difficult to concentrate when she was near, but it was different with Rosetta. My heart didn't pound madly, and there was no great urge to kiss her, but the conversation was agreeable and pleasant. We had things to talk about, and I admired the way she carried herself. The fact that we *could* be together was definitely a plus, too.

"My wedding day was a much smaller affair. My mother's family isn't very large, and I didn't want the pressure of preparing the event for too many guests. It was nice, though. I have no regrets," she said, meeting my gaze. "What was yours like?"

I ran my hand through my beard. I never regretted my three children, but marrying Miranda had been a mistake. Early on, I hadn't realized how flighty and disturbed she was. She'd hidden her true nature well, and I'd been too stupid in love to see the signs. I couldn't tell Rosetta that. She wouldn't understand my harsh feelings toward my dead wife. CJ was the only other person in the world that knew—and would ever know the reason why I felt the way I did.

"Ours was quite large—not like this, though. I reckon we had close to four hundred in attendance. It was in autumn, very much like today."

"Mine was a spring wedding, but I see the appeal of wedding after the harvest, when the leaves are brilliant and the days are cool." The line of men and women on the other side of Rosetta swelled and she was forced to squeeze against me. "I'm sorry," she said, blushing.

The close proximity to her didn't set my blood on fire the way any contact with CJ did. I kind of liked the lack of feeling. It was very safe, and I was able to remain clear headed. I chuckled. "No worries. I don't mind."

Her face lit up, and I quickly returned my gaze to the horses.

The crowd whooped and hollered. David's arm was raised over head as he crossed the finish line first.

"Did you expect him to win?" Rosetta asked as we left the railing with everyone else.

"David had a mighty fine team. It certainly doesn't surprise me." I glanced over and saw that Rosetta was paying close attention to what I said. She really was a pleasant woman to be around. "Do you want to get a hamburger with me?"

"Of course, Joshua."

Guilt flared in my chest. Somehow, I had to get over CJ West— and what better way to do it than with another woman.

19

CJ

I sat at the picnic table and took a bite of the burger, not really tasting the food. My stomach had been tight ever since we'd parked at the huge Amish party. If you asked me, it was a strange way to celebrate a wedding the next day. The community had gathered to watch a competition where horses pulled heavy loads across the finish line. The evening breeze was chilly and I zipped up my hoody, spying on the Amish all around. Groups of small children raced through the legs of the adults, and small pockets of teens mingled. For the most part, the groups were split by sex—even the children. The men stuck together, as did the women. There was a volleyball game going on beside the road. The girls batting the ball back and forth looked like a bouquet of colorful flowers, with their dresses a rainbow of blues, greens, pinks, and purples.

The two women sitting across from me were in deep conversation, but the baby on one of the women's shoulders gurgled noises and blew bubbles at me. I made faces back at him and sipped my cola. To say I felt out of place was an understatement. Almost everyone present was Amish, except for a few drivers strolling in the crowd.

A tug on my arm snapped my head down. Staring up at me was the cutest little girl I'd ever seen. She couldn't have been more than three years old. Her brown eyes were as large as saucers and her cheeks were rosy. She wore a brown sweater that matched her dress, and several wisps of blonde hair flared out from her white cap.

She rattled off a sentence that I didn't understand. I glanced around and saw that no one was paying any attention to us. "I'm sorry. I don't know what you're saying."

The child backed up and pointed at a tricycle. Standing a few feet away was a boy about the same age, holding onto to a tiny red wagon. The boy stepped closer and lifted the tongue of the wagon and stared hard at me with a very serious look on his round face.

"Oh. Do you want me to hook it up for you two?" I swung my leg over the bench and knelt down between the kids.

They nodded vigorously and I bent to get a better look at the clasped peg on the tricycle. It was ironic that these children singled me out to help them when there were hundreds of their own people all around. As I glanced over my shoulder, I realized that I appeared to be only other person there who was alone. Everyone else was preoccupied with someone else.

The kids must have thought I looked bored or something. I got to work and squeezed the clasp to open it. Then I pulled the wagon until the holes lined up and slid the peg down, closing the clasp. Once the wagon was connected, the boy jumped onto the tricycle and the girl took her place in the wagon. As the boy peddled her away, the little brown-dressed girl looked back and called out, "Thank you!"

Her voice was stilted, as if she didn't speak English very often, but she'd recognized me for an outsider and spoke to me in my language. I watched until the children disappeared around the leaves of a burnt orange bush. I wondered where their parents were, and then a tickling in my heart made me turn my head. I caught sight of Joshua at a picnic table—and right there beside him was Rosetta.

I ducked behind the bush, feeling like an idiot hiding from him. But the fear of him seeing me there—all alone—while he was once again in the company of the woman, who he said was only his friend, made my head spin.

What was he doing here anyway?

Of course, I already knew the answer. He was at the wedding for the same reason as Katherine and her husband, Joseph—to escape from Blood Rock for a little while and have some fun. My cheeks burned and my blood boiled. Joshua worked fast. Only hours earlier, I'd been in his arms. He'd kissed me passionately and done other things…

I shook my head. *Dammit—why did I come?*

"CJ, are you all right?"

I jumped sideways. It was Katherine. Her hand rested on my arm and her eyes were pools of concern.

I glanced back to where Joshua had been, and he and Rosetta were gone. Holding my breath, I scanned the area. When I failed to locate the pair, I returned my gaze to Katherine.

"I'm fine." She wasn't convinced. After all, I was practically hiding in a bush. "I just, ah, was going to make a phone call." I pulled my cellphone from my back pocket and held it up, grateful that I had thought of something sort of reasonable to say.

Her face still twitched with worry. "I was looking for you."

"Why?"

"This is your first time at such a crowded event. I feared that you might feel a little lost."

This kind woman, who hasn't had a proper date night in many years, is why you're here, I reminded myself.

"Don't worry about me. I'm just taking it all in," I lied.

Katherine had on a pretty lavender dress. Her skin glowed and her eyes twinkled. She was enjoying herself. She pointed toward a white-sided barn. "Over there, the other drivers are gathered. You may enjoy their company." She smiled encouragingly and I pressed my lips together and nodded back. She pulled a piece of paper from the pocket of her smock and handed it to me. "Here's the address for where you'll be staying. Joseph and I will take a buggy ride back to my cousins' home tonight. You're welcome to leave whenever you're ready." She tilted her head. "You look tired."

I rubbed my fingers together. "I am a little. I'll probably head out in a while." She turned to go and I stopped her. "What time does the wedding begin tomorrow?"

"Nine o'clock in the morning, but most of the English folk arrive around eleven or so—that way they don't have to suffer through the long service, which they're unaccustomed to."

"How long exactly does it take?" I asked slowly.

"Around three hours. It will be conducted by the local bishop and ministers in German." She gestured to the large white metal building across the driveway. "The service and supper will be held in there."

"Is it all right if I come when it begins?" Her brows furrowed, and I quickly added, "I'm curious about your weddings. I'd like to experience the entire celebration."

Katherine swayed closer. "Of course, you may come early, but don't say I didn't warn you." She chuckled as she walked away. She barely took a few strides when a couple of other ladies joined her, talking rapidly. Her husband was nowhere in sight. I shook my head. So much for date night.

I left the cover of the bushes and collected my food off of the table, only to throw the plate away in the first trash can I passed. Seeing Joshua and Rosetta had thoroughly ruined my appetite, and I was fighting my anger. Joshua had asked me to consider becoming

Amish, and I had basically laughed at him. I got it that he didn't want to leave his culture, especially with three kids who would be affected by such a drastic change. He was a farmer and had ties with a community that would surely shun him if he left their order. The fact that he was moving on with a respectable Amish woman wasn't surprising. The speed of it was another story.

I yawned and pressed my finger to my temple. A small headache still throbbed there. I needed to take some ibuprofen and turn in early. Maybe I would read for a little while. That might get my mind off Joshua.

I hadn't gone very far when someone called my name out. I cringed and reluctantly turned to look. It was Martha. She was a driver I'd met a few months ago. Her husband sat in a lawn chair next to her. They were both gray-haired and jovial people.

I diverted my course and stopped in front of them. "Hello. It's nice to see you both again."

"My dear. How are you feeling? I heard all about what Caleb Johnson did to you." She shook her head. "It stops my heart when I think that he turned out to be the murderer." She shook her head and her lips were pinched. "I still have a difficult time sleeping at night. I can only imagine what your dreams are like. He really fooled us all."

Her words made me feel a little dizzy. I worked to lock my legs in place and stay focused on Martha's face. What she said had affected me—the nightmares were almost too much to bear at times. I had a long way to go to be fully healed from the ordeal.

"I'm doing all right, but I try not to think about it too much."

"Take the hint, Martha," Dick said.

Martha looked horrified. "I'm sorry, CJ. I meant nothing by it—really."

"I know. It's not you, it's me." I glanced around again, hoping I wouldn't see Joshua. "Are you going to the wedding?"

She elbowed Dick. "How many of these Amish marriages have we witnessed?"

Dick shrugged. "Reckon, maybe twenty or more."

"Anyway, too many to count. We don't personally know the bride or groom. We just drove some of the community over." She shot me a knowing look. "I see you got wrangled into driving someone here. Are you planning to attend the ceremony?"

"I was thinking about it. Is it really that bad?"

Martha bumped her husband again and snorted. "If you do go, bring a cushion, and something to read."

I chuckled. "Thanks for the advice."

"We'll see you for suppertime—we never miss the food." Martha winked.

"I'm glad I'll have people to sit with." I took a step back. "I'm going to turn in for the night. Sounds like I'll need a good rest to get through tomorrow."

"If you need anything, we're staying at the Motel 8 in town."

We said our goodbyes and I made my way in between the dozens of buggies parked in the field to reach my car. Occasionally, I stopped to pet the nose of a friendly horse seeking attention, but I walked quickly, praying that I wouldn't run into Joshua.

As much as I wanted to see what an Amish wedding was really like, I realized it would be a big mistake for me to go. Joshua would surely see me and I didn't want that. He would probably think I was stalking him or something. Besides, if I was going to get him out of my mind, I had to avoid running into him—at least until I got a grip on my emotions.

Which would probably be never.

20

JOSHUA

The buggy waiting for me was harnessed to an impressive bay gelding. I took a moment to admire the horse's arched neck and strong muscles.

"He's beautiful," Rosetta sighed.

I returned my attention to her. "Yes, he is." I shifted my weight between feet. "Are you catching a ride with the Blood Rock group to their accommodations?"

She nodded and pointed to the van parked on the road. "They're leaving now."

"I'll see you in the morning." It was an awkward moment. We'd spent the evening walking and talking together. There was an implication that we were already a couple, but my heart just wasn't in it.

"I look forward to it." She hesitated, and then smiled. It was almost a schoolgirl expression, full of anticipation.

I drew in a sobering breath when Rosetta left and hurried toward the van.

"You and Rosetta are hitting it off well," Lester commented as we climbed into the buggy.

Ester squeezed into the cramped space and I opened the sliding window, resting my arm outside it. "She's a good woman, but I fear things are being rushed a bit. It's only been a year since I became a widow. My concentration is on my children and farming the new property."

"Well, when Rosetta has her mind set on something…or someone, she always gets her way," Esther spoke up. Her thin lips were turned up in a smirk.

"You know her, then?" I asked.

She shrugged. "I spent some time in her home community when I was growing up. She mentioned her interest in you to me the other day."

I looked out the window. If there was one thing I hated, it was a gossipy woman. Esther was the worst kind—one that would betray another's confidence. I really didn't see how a nice fellow like Lester ended up with a woman like her.

The short trip to the driveway leading to the cabin I was staying in was quiet, except for the sound of hooves striking the pavement. As darkness fully enveloped the countryside, my thoughts drifted to CJ. Was she already packing her belongings, or was she possibly spending the evening with the Englisher named Nathan?

The buggy came to an abrupt stop and I said my goodbyes, before I grabbed my bag from the floorboard. The horse followed the circular drive and was heading back onto the roadway. Lester's hand shot out the window and I waved back.

I stood in a stand of draping maple trees, studying the two log cabins. They were side by side and exactly the same, except a light glowed from the window in the cabin to left. There were boots and smaller black tennis shoes placed neatly to the side of the door and a black coat hung on the peg. That cabin was already taken, so I made my way up the porch steps to the doorway leading into the one that was dark. I was told the door would be unlocked, so I wasted no time pushing it open and walking in. I was exhausted and hoped that I would be able to fall quickly into a dreamless sleep. The last thing I needed was another lost night's rest due to images of CJ dancing around in my head.

There was just enough light shining through the little window that I was able to find the gas light, hanging above the kitchen counter. The cabin appeared to have only a couple of rooms, so when the light was lit it should illuminate the space well enough.

I pulled the box from my pocket and struck the match. The room lit up, but only for an instant. Something heavy struck my shoulder and the side of my head. I stumbled into the wall, blinking and fighting for balance.

"What the—"

"Joshua?" someone whispered.

I knew that voice. My heart froze and I caught my breath as I turned and looked up.

"CJ? What the hell are you doing here?" I regretted cussing, but I was in such a state of shock…and pain, I could hardly think straight.

"I'm sorry!" She rushed to the sink and began running water over a towel. "I thought someone was breaking in."

I took a few steps and slunk onto the couch. A couple of blankets were strewn across the cushions and I guessed CJ had been lying there when I'd entered the cabin, frightening her. After the attack she'd endured not so long ago, it made sense that she'd strike first, and ask questions later. She crossed the wood floor at a jog and dropped down beside me on the couch. Gingerly, she pressed the cold cloth to the side of my head.

"Do you need to the go to the hospital? I can locate one on my phone and take you there." Her voice was still panicked.

I groaned and shifted my position. "I don't think that will be necessary. My shoulder took the brunt of it." I rubbed the place she'd struck, and before I could stop her, she started to unbutton my shirt.

Even though she'd nearly knocked me out only a moment before, a rush of adrenaline coursed through my veins when she touched me. I pulled back, suddenly panicked myself. "Stop that. What are you doing?" I gently intercepted her hands, but she'd already unlatched one of the buttons.

She ignored me and pulled the material down, revealing my shoulder. "I want to see how much damage I did." She sucked in a shaky breath. "Oh. You're going to have an enormous bruise. Let me see if there's any ice in the fridge."

I snatched her arm and she fell back onto the couch before she was able to get away. "CJ, why are you here, in my cabin?" My mind raced with the impossibility her presence, but the feel of her skin beneath my fingertips told me she was all too real.

She sat up and her pretty green eyes narrowed. "This is my cabin. I've been here for over an hour, and I was almost asleep when you barged in."

I inhaled, trying to keep my voice steady, but my impatience was growing. "You aren't supposed to be here."

"Why, because you didn't invite me? Or maybe because you were planning a romantic night with your new girlfriend. Huh, is that it?"

Her words pounded the inside of my head, and I barked out a laugh. "As you can see yourself, Rosetta isn't with me, and there were no such romantic plans. You're the only woman I've been romantic with since my wife died." CJ drew back, her eyes widening. The innocent look of dawning on her face jolted my senses. I wanted to pull her against me and kiss those parted lips, but I fought the impulse and softened my voice. "Lester invited me along to the wedding. The groom is my nephew, and I thought it would be a way to put some distance between you and I—so that we could begin healing."

She chewed her bottom lip and the wind picked up beyond the cabin's walls. There was a pattering of taps on the tin roof as dry leaves pelted the building. I stared back at CJ, too cautious to say anything.

She swallowed and licked her lips. "Katherine and Joseph needed a ride. Their driver was sick, and they hadn't had a vacation without the kids since they were married." Her mouth dropped open. "Can you believe that?" I wasn't surprised. I hadn't been away alone with my wife once we began having children, either. When I didn't say anything, she went on. "I felt sorry for her and volunteered to drive them at the last minute."

I finally found my voice. "Where's your car?"

Her face tightened with a look of annoyance at the question. "It's behind the cabin. There's a gravel area, and that's where the lady—don't ask me her name, because I've already forgotten—told me to park."

I leaned back. There was only a slight burning sensation at the side of my head, and a dull ache in my shoulder. I absorbed what she told me and wondered at the unlikely chance that we ended up here together, alone in the same cabin.

"I'll collect my stuff and get a hotel room in town," CJ said. She wiggled her arm away from me and stood up.

I rose with her. "You don't have to do that. It's nighttime, and you're in an unfamiliar place."

She tilted her head. "It's really not a big deal. I can just hop in my car and use the GPS to find a place to go. That's one of the good things about having technology in my life—it's really easy."

It felt like she'd slapped me. I stepped back and watched her gather up her belongings, shoving things into a duffle bag. My gaze followed her every move. She wore the same type of tank top she'd had on the day we went riding, only this time, it was plain to see that she wasn't wearing a bra beneath it. I did intrude on her privacy, so her sleeping attire was completely acceptable under the circumstances. She was in such a hurry to leave that I doubted she even realized how desirable I found her.

CJ zipped the bag and picked up her hooded sweatshirt off of the chair. The inside of the cabin was small, but cozy. Quilts draped over the backs of the chairs and the exposed logs and chinking gave the room a rustic feel that was very inviting.

Before CJ was able to pull the material over her head I said, "Stop. Don't go."

She paused. "What will your people think if you spend the night with an English woman, Joshua? Believe me, the way news travels in these communities, they will find out about it."

My heart leaped into my throat. She was right, but at that moment, I didn't really care enough about being found out to push her out the door. Recklessness took hold of my head, and my heart. "If you drive off at this hour, I'll worry about your safety all night long. Something might happen to you."

"I suppose you can leave and stay with someone else," she ventured.

The thought had crossed my mind, but a dozen reasons made me think twice. "Everyone's turning in by now. This community is bursting at the seams with guests for the wedding." I leveled a firm look at CJ. "It's best if we stay here together for the night. Early in the morning, you can leave with your car, and maybe visit one of the restaurants for breakfast. There's a lot of places to shop for country crafts and antiques to keep you busy until after the wedding and reception."

"You have it all figured out, don't you?" Her eyes were accusing. I inadvertently took a step forward, reaching out to her, but she jumped away. "Sure, we can have sex in the dark, and before the sun rises, I'll sneak away, so you don't get into trouble."

I shook my head roughly. "That never entered my mind. We have already discussed our relationship. You won't become Amish, and I can't go English. I'm trying to do the right thing here. I'll sleep on the couch—and you can have the bed. If you want, I'll be the one to leave first thing in the morning."

She slumped and rubbed her cheek. "I feel like I'm stuck in a rerun of a bad comedy sitcom. Sure, whatever. I'm too tired to go looking for someplace else to stay anyway. You're the one who stands to get into trouble, not me."

"It's just one night. We can survive that," I assured her.

But deep down, I knew just how difficult it would be for both of us.

21

CJ

I closed my eyes and listened to the wind pummeling the cabin's walls and rattling the glass pane in the window. I had the flashlight on the nightstand next to the bed. If for some reason I had to make a quick exit, I didn't want to have to fool with lighting the lamps. I rolled again, and stared across the room at the couch. I could just make out the silhouette of Joshua's form in the dark. My belly churned with icy butterflies, and I groaned quietly into a pillow.

I should have just left. It would be a heck of a lot less torturous to have been driving around in the middle of the night, than to be trapped inside the cute little cabin with a man I wanted to punch and make love to, all at the same time.

What kind of a bizarre coincidence was it that Joshua ended up being told to stay in the exact same cabin that I was given directions to? The odds were a million to one, and yet, here we were. After the fear of an intruder, and the initial shock that I'd almost knocked out none other than Joshua Miller, the realization that he was alone had hit me like a tornado. Yes, Rosetta was a proper Amish woman, and he was pretending to be an honorable Amish man, yet they still could have somehow arranged a hookup at the cabin. They were grown adults after all, and both had been widowed. It was hard to believe anyone in the community would have noticed or cared much.

For whatever reason, Joshua had arrived here alone, and that gave me a tingle of joy that maybe he wasn't as into Rosetta as I originally thought he was. But what good would that realization do me? We both knew we couldn't be together, and the irony was that we both came here, trying to get over each other.

What I really wanted to do was slip off my clothes and join him on the couch. My skin grew hot and I closed my eyes. I was sure he wouldn't tell me to go back to the bed. His emotions for me were just as raw as mine were for him—I'd bet money on it. I'd seen the way his eyes had racked over me, like a hungry wolf.

True to his word, he hadn't made any attempt to seduce me. Now I tossed and turned, aching for him, almost to the point that I was about to grab my things and sleep in the car.

I wasn't that immature, I shouted to myself. I listened carefully and could hear Joshua's steady breaths. He was asleep. If he could ignore my presence, then I would ignore his.

I pressed my gritty eyes closed tightly. It took a while, but eventually waves of heaviness invaded my mind. With a long sigh, I finally drifted off to sleep.

I was trapped in a dark space. I couldn't see and I groped along the floor, trying to find the door. The footsteps behind me forced me to move faster. A kick to my side brought me flat against the boards, knocking the wind from my lungs.

I couldn't breathe.

And then there was a sick chuckling sound. "I'm going to kill you, CJ West."

I screamed.

"Wake up, CJ. It's just a nightmare!"

The voice in my ear was solid and loud. I fluttered my eyes open as the dream dispersed into fuzziness.

"Shh. It's all right. You're awake now." Joshua rocked me against his strong chest, like I was one of his kids.

I felt stupid, and tried to pull back. "I'm sorry." I mumbled. "Sometimes I have intense dreams. Did I wake you?"

He continued to hold me close, and I inhaled the scent of him. Leather, horses, and fields of hay filled my nose. The ache I'd felt earlier surged to life in my groin and I sagged against him. Now that I was in his arms, I trembled, knowing what was to come.

"You screamed—nearly scared me to death. I thought something had happened." His breath mingled with mine. "Don't ever say you're sorry, though. You have every reason to experience ill dreams from time to time after what you've been through." His hand found the back of my head, and his fingers threaded my hair, massaging my scalp. His voice was husky. "I'm just glad I was here to wake you…"

My pulse fluttered. We were both holding our breath, when the need inside of me became too great. I pressed my breasts to the solid wall of his chest, and touched his lips with mine. At first, he didn't respond, but I didn't care. I was right where I wanted to be, and even if it was only for one night, it was worth it. This was my goodbye to Joshua Miller.

I trailed my fingers along the bulging muscles of his arm, every so lightly, enjoying the way he tensed at my touch. He was trying to hold back—do the right thing, as he called it—but his rapid breathing, and the thumping of his heart gave him away.

"God, you're beautiful," he rasped. "This feels so right."

Joshua finally let go and his mouth opened to mine. He climbed slowly over me, pinning me into the mattress. I wrapped my legs around his waist and arched against him. He groaned into my ear, and then nipped my lower lip. His need was as great as my own. He knew he was making a mistake, but he didn't care—just like me. We needed one more time in each other's arms before going our separate ways.

His busy hands pulled the tank top over my head, and he trailed his tongue over the curve of my jaw, down to the hollow of my neck. I shivered deliciously as his mouth moved lower and his fingers played over my breasts until his lips closed over a nipple. I moaned, more than eager to give myself to him.

"I can't get enough of you," he groaned. His words were full of the same desperate need that was driving me crazy. I tugged on his shirt and several buttons popped off. He didn't seem to notice. He lifted up just enough to shrug the material off and toss it aside. His pants joined the pile on the floor and I inhaled sharply as he stood naked above me. His body was long, lean, and strong. I sat up and moved my palms over his taut, quivering stomach. He gasped and I embraced him, digging my fingers into his back. When his lips returned to mine, he controlled his desire, kissing me with slow tenderness that made my muscles tense. I felt his hard bulge against my thigh and I rubbed against it. He was holding back, and I was losing my mind.

He pulled back and stared down. I saw a glint of wetness in those blue eyes. His voice shook. "Is this what you really want, CJ?"

"Please." I laced my hands behind his head and tried to bring him down to me. "Don't stop."

He grunted, bringing his face only an inch from mine. "You're killing me, you know that?"

I wouldn't think about what the next day would bring. I just couldn't. Soon enough, I would move someplace far away, and Joshua would be holding Rosetta in his arms—but not tonight. The powers of the universe had brought us together. Or perhaps God had a sense of humor. Either way, Joshua and I would have this one night. And at the moment, that's all that mattered.

"Joshua." I peeked up under my lashes. "I. Want. You."

Those three words were enough.

In a swift motion, he pulled my panties off and he grasped the curves of my waist. Slowly, ever so slowly, he lifted my hips. Our eyes locked, and then he lowered me until I was astride him. My muscles clamped and trembled around him.

I sighed into his mouth.

I might regret this in the morning, but right now I would revel in every minute I had with the handsome Amish man.

Because this one night was all we had.

22

JOSHUA

A rooster crowed in the distance. I was still half asleep, but I couldn't help inhaling CJ's scent from the pillow. I buried my face into it to fill my nostrils, imprinting the wildflower smell in my mind forever. I felt better than I had in years. I stretched and covered a yawn. My groin throbbed as memories flooded back from the night before. The arousal would have been welcome if we had more time, but people would soon be rising for the wedding. The urge to love CJ again was too great, though. I rolled over, reaching for her. When my hands couldn't find her, my eyes popped open, and I searched the muted early morning light.

My skin prickled and I bolted upright. Her duffle bag was gone.

I threw my legs over the side of the bed and hurried my pants on. Standing up, I strode to the back door and flung it open. CJ's car was nowhere in sight. She must have risen at the break of dawn and snuck out. I rubbed my face and closed the door behind me.

I had so many things to say to her, but now, that conversation had to wait until after the wedding and we were home again. Making love to CJ had opened my eyes and my heart to the truth. I loved the

English woman, and I wasn't going to let her get away—even if it meant changes were on the wind. Some things were worth sacrifice, and love certainly was a good reason.

With renewed energy, I fetched a fresh shirt from my bag. Now that I'd made my decision, contentment washed over me.

I just had to be patient for a little while longer.

I shook the groom's hand and tipped my hat to the bride. There were two young people, a girl and boy pair, on either side of them. This was their wedding party. The greeting line was long, and the autumn breeze warmer than it had been the day before. I glanced up. The sun shined through a smattering of plump clouds.

Making small talk with the other men, I slowly made my way to an empty space on the bench on the male side of the building. The women were quietly filing into the benches on the other side. I kept my head down, trying not to make eye contact with Rosetta. Still, I felt her hot gaze directed at me when I looked up. She smiled and I reluctantly returned the favor. Rosetta was intelligent and sound minded. She was also tall and lithe, with an attractive face. If what Esther had said about Rosetta's personality was true, the bishop's niece would have no problem finding another suiter. Yet, the entire situation was disquieting. I didn't want to hurt the woman's feelings, but it was inevitable. Soon they would all know the truth.

I quickly turned the other way and filled the time by watching people take their seats. This metal building was usually a place where the wooden pallets made by the bride's family business were stored. But today, it was the site of a wedding. Smells from the upcoming reception were already drifting in through the sliding doors. Supper would be served in the adjacent barn by dozens of young women and girls from around the community. The food and dinner conversation really were the best part of the day. Weddings were happy affairs for my people. It was one of the rare times when everyone lightened up a bit and really enjoyed themselves. It was also a time to see old friends and make new ones. Even so, I recalled attending an English wedding years ago. I'd been invited to my driver's wedding, and since several others from the community were going, I joined too. The event had been filled with alcohol and rowdy behavior by the guests. It was so different from what I was used to, I vowed to never attend one again. Of course, my relationship with CJ had made me begin to question my own ways. As more people took their seats, I couldn't help but notice how different our customs really were. Here, families couldn't sit together. The men were on one side, and the women on the other. Their children were separated. Usually the boys sat with their fathers, and the girls with their mothers. A few men had baby daughters sleeping on their shoulders, though.

The benches in the back were reserved for any Englishers invited to the wedding. Drivers, neighbors, and business acquaintances sat there, separated from the Amish. Rarely, did they arrive at the beginning of the service. Three to three and a half hours of sitting on a hard bench was too much for most outsiders. It was expected that they'd show up a couple of hours later, catching just the last hour or so of the ceremony.

When my gaze passed over the back of the building, I froze. CJ was sitting there, all alone, with her hands folded in her lap. Her curly hair was pulled off her face and swept up in silver barrette. She wore a mint green colored dress that matched her eyes, and that barely covered her knees. My heart stilled at the sight of her. I wanted to go to her, but I didn't dare move a muscle. This was a very special day for two people and their families. I wouldn't do anything to disrupt the event in any way. If I followed my gut and joined CJ, it would definitely cause a stir.

Our eyes met for an instant, and she looked away. I wondered why she had decided to come to the wedding in the first place. Especially at the very beginning of the ceremony. I continued to watch her, hoping she'd grace me with a glance, but she was avoiding me. My neck tensed and I turned back around. Was it possible that she was still angry about having to keep our night together a secret? She would have to understand the need to do so. Still, she had left earlier than even I wanted her to. We could have spent a little more time together before we parted ways for the rest of the day. I could have told her about my decision, and calmed her own worries.

We probably wouldn't have gotten much talking done, though. My face heated and I rubbed my mouth with my fingertips. I caught Rosetta's glance, and cold guilt doused the fire in my belly. If CJ saw Rosetta with me, it would definitely rile her, but there wasn't much I could do about it at the moment. The day would be long, and the Amish woman would seek me out, even if I tried to ignore her. I was certain of it.

I was thankful for the distraction of the hymnals being handed out. I picked mine up and began to sing with the others.

23

CJ

The song was the melancholiest I'd ever heard—and it was in German. I wasn't exactly surprised by that, but I hadn't thought about the language issue before I'd arrived, either. A gray-haired woman on the bench ahead of me reached back and handed me a hymnal. I took it and mouthed, *thank you*. She nodded and returned to singing.

The hymnal was in German too. I stifled a yawn and listened to the congregation. The men would sing a verse, with their loud, lower tones, and then the women would pick up the next verse in higher voices. At times, the entire congregation would join together. They sang in harmony well, but the drone of the song was so rigid and boring, I felt my eyelids becoming heavy.

I sucked in a quiet breath, filling my head with oxygen to revive my senses. My eyes drifted from time to time to the back of Joshua's head, even though I tried really hard to ignore him. His back was straight, and like all the other men, he wore a black jacket and hat. The look of longing he'd shot me earlier was startling. I wasn't expecting him to pay any attention to me at all. Like a dutiful one-night stand, I'd risen early enough to sneak away while he was still sound asleep. It was better that way. It would have been annoying to have him rushing me out the door after the passion between us the night before had ended. And oh, was there a lot of passion…

I blushed, and the song ended. A long-bearded man stood in front of the room and began to speak. His words were soft, and of course, in German. The building was filled to the max, and yet the crowd was silent and unmoving. Even the children sat like little statues, replicas of the adults around them.

Within minutes, my butt began hurting and I shifted my weight to change the pressure points. I re-crossed my legs and spied on the Amish people around me. There was an elderly couple sitting further down on the bench. They were English, too, but the three of us were the only non-Amish people in the building. I was warned about the discomfort I'd have to endure if I came early, but unlike the other English guests who might arrive later, I had desperately wanted to see what an entire Amish wedding was really like. Maybe it was my relationship with Joshua, or perhaps I could attribute me stubbornly being here to my intense curiosity about most new things.

Katherine had waved when I'd first stepped from the sunlight into the dim interior of the building, but before I could make my way to her, a stern-faced lady had shuffled me to the benches in the very back. It was probably for the best. I had a good vantage point to observe the comings and goings of everyone. Seeing that the community was split into two sides, with the women and men sitting separately, I was relieved I hadn't accidentally sat in area restricted to the masculine population. Then I had watched Joshua stroll in with the other men and take his seat. Images of him standing in all his naked glory had sprung to life in my wicked mind.

It was too much for me to keep eye contact with him. I might have acted like a wanton slut the night before, but now, my confidence was gone. Joshua didn't belong to me. I had known that sleeping with him was foolish, but for once in my life, I'd followed my heart instead of my head. I had always been the girl who thought everything out. I wasn't carefree or fun. My entire life had been governed by being responsible. Well...last night, I'd finally let loose. Having sex, multiple times, with the Amish widower was the most freeing thing I'd ever done. It was exciting while it had lasted, but now it was over.

I'd always understood the drastic differences in our societies, and observing the Amish people on that morning—how the men and women were separated, and how stoic they all were on what should have been a happy occasion, made me even more certain that leaving Joshua's farm was the only thing to do. If I stayed, I might actually fall in love with Joshua—and I wouldn't admit that to anyone else, even Serenity. From the beginning it was an impossible, forbidden romance, but Joshua was like a drug. If I didn't break ties completely with him, I'd be destroyed. Because in the end, he would settle down with Rosetta or a woman just like her, and I wasn't hanging around to see that happen.

The minister droned on for a while longer, and then the congregation broke into another dull song. I changed positions again and cracked my neck. After the song ended, a different man stood up. This guy was older. Gray peppered his beard and his voice was loud and sharp. He walked back and forth in front of the congregation with an air of authority and purpose that the other man didn't possess. I would bet that he was their bishop.

Every once in a while, an English word escaped his lips, and I'd perk up, hopeful that he might begin speaking fully in a language I understood. A three-hour service was rough, but not having any idea what was being said was really torturous. Occasionally, a woman would leave the building with a baby in her arms or a toddler in tow. Sometimes Katherine would check in on me, with a quick smile over her shoulder. At one point, the back of my neck tingled and I searched the crowd until I found the source of my discomfort. It was Rosetta. She had finally seen me. Her face was clear of any noticeable reaction, but her eyes were wide and troubled. I didn't like her, for the sole reason that she'd set her eyes on the man I wanted, and I was ashamed I felt that way toward a woman I barely knew. She was the perfect match for Joshua, not me.

I forced a polite smile on my face and held Rosetta's gaze. She was the first to look away. I nibbled my fingernail as my stomach churned. I was ready to go home and begin packing. Unfortunately, there was no way I was exiting now. I'd stuck it out for two and a half hours—I could handle a little while longer, even with Rosetta's occasional glare.

Everyone slid to their knees, turned and clasped their hands on the benches. I followed suit, but I remained seated for the bishop's prayer. After a few minutes, the man paused and everyone returned to their seats. Joshua sought me out, but again, I avoided his gaze when our eyes briefly met.

Just as the bishop stopped talking and another acapella song began, about a dozen English people joined me on the back bench. Martha spotted me and guided her husband to slide next to me on the seat.

"Have you been here since the beginning?" she whispered into my ear.

I nodded, grinning back at her.

"Poor thing," she said, patting my thigh.

While the song droned on, the bride and groom stood up in the front and center of the room. There was a couple on each side of them. I only guessed that it was the wedding party, because the girls wore white aprons over their plain blue dresses, just like the bride. There was nothing unique about the shy-looking bride. She was short and wore no makeup. But all that was forgotten when she looked up at the young man beside her. Deep love was there for everyone to see.

When the music stopped, the bishop spoke to the couple. I craned my neck to see and hear better. This part of the ceremony was a quick affair. There was no kiss at the end, or thunderous applause from the crowd. The bride and groom's departure from the building was just as quiet and unassuming as their entrance. I glanced at my phone. Three hours and ten minutes. I figured the sermon alone was over an hour long. Thankful for the opportunity to finally stand, I stretched and picked up my purse.

"You'll sit with us, won't you, CJ?" Martha asked.

I glanced around. Joshua had disappeared in the sea of dark coats. "I was thinking about heading back to my car and taking a nap. I didn't sleep well last night." I wondered what Martha would think if she knew I was sleep deprived because I'd been up all night fooling around with Joshua.

"Nonsense. My girl, you just sat through an entire Amish wedding ceremony. Not many Englishers can claim that achievement. The best part of the day is supper—and you're not going to miss it."

I snorted, holding up my hands. "Okay, okay. You've talked me into it."

I followed Dick and Martha through the doorway and into the bright sunlight. I put on my sunglasses and exhaled at the beauty of the autumn countryside. The trees were washed out browns, oranges, and yellows. The sky was a brilliant blue. Somewhere nearby there was a fire burning, and I inhaled the sweet scent of wood burning. A group of children ran by, and I recognized the little girl and boy I'd helped with their tricycle and wagon the night before. They didn't see me, and continued their mad dash for the building where Katherine had explained that the reception would take place.

A long line of black and brown horses was tied to the fence, and the smell of their sweaty fur was sharp on the air. I had another moment of feeling like I was in different world as Martha guided me through the throng of people. The reserved behavior from earlier had disappeared. Everyone was talkative and fairly animated. The women's colorful dresses collided with the white shirts, stark black pants, and jackets that the men wore. Some spoke English, but most continued speaking in the German dialect.

A hand grasped my shoulder, and I jumped, spinning around.

"How are you fairing after that?" Katherine asked. Her face was bright and well rested. She seemed to be really enjoying her time away from the kids. Joseph was a few feet away, talking to another man. No surprise there.

The usual reply, like saying it had been a beautiful ceremony or that the bride's dress was gorgeous, just wasn't fitting, so I decided to be as honest as I could.

"It was such a unique experience. I'm glad I insisted on attending the entire service," I said.

Katherine's smile was radiant. "I'm happy you're enjoying yourself, and I see Martha has taken you under her wing. After supper, we must be on our way."

"Are you ready to go home?" I asked, somewhat cautiously.

"Oh, yes. I've had a marvelous time, but I'm sure the children are missing me by now," she replied.

Her voice had shaken a little. She was actually missing her kids, after only one night apart. It was hard to fathom that she was ready to return to the care, cooking, and cleaning of a half dozen kids. If I had my own family someday, maybe I'd fully understand the reason for her anxiety.

Martha led the group of Englishers through the entrance, where a girl quickly showed us the table that we were supposed to sit at. Once again, it was in the furthest back corner of the crowded room.

I didn't mind. Our server girls were friendly, and I liked sitting in a place where I could observe what was happening without being the center of attention.

I watched people stream in from the open doors, and then turned my attention to the tabletops. There were little paper name tags in cursive resting on some of the dinner plates. Husbands, wives, and families were seated together, and I recognized a group of Blood Rock citizens filling one of the nearby tables.

My heart skipped a beat when Joshua walked in. His head swiveled around until he spotted the lone table with all the regularly dressed folk. When his eyes settled on me, his face was tense and he frowned slightly.

A large bowl of chicken thighs appeared and I was grateful for the opportunity to drop my gaze. When I looked up. Joshua was already sitting at the Blood Rock table—and right across from him was Rosetta. Since she was facing me, I saw her tilt her head and say something to him.

Anger flared in my belly, but I didn't have time to dwell on my bitter emotions. Another equally large bowl appeared, nearly overflowing with mashed potatoes. The serving girls filled our glasses with water or iced tea as more bowls arrived. Soon my plate was nearly full, but I did my best to squeeze in the green beans, coleslaw, and noodles. On the tables, at intervals of about two feet, there were flower bouquets of pink and white roses, and in between those were flickering candles. Where the ceremony room had been subdued and colorless, the reception was decorated just enough to be festive. In the front corner of the room, a three-tiered cake sat prettily on a round table, and another table was stacked high with brightly wrapped gift boxes. I spotted a chainsaw, with an enormous bow attached to it, and I had to control my mirth—only at an Amish wedding would you see such a gift.

The cacophony of sound consisted of clinking dishes and rapid talking. The mixture of English and German was distracting, but after a few bites of my delicious meal, I got used to the jumble of their words. Martha did her best to include me in the conversation between the drivers, but I couldn't help being a bit aloof. My heart was numb, and it took all my wits to focus at all.

A lot of people had it much worse off than me, so I didn't want to wallow in self-pity. I'd been bombarded with a string of bad stuff in my life lately. In the past six months, my long-term boyfriend cheated on me, and then dumped me for a college girl. I moved to Blood Rock to move past that heartache, and along came Joshua Miller, a completely unavailable guy, who I couldn't resist. Then I was kidnapped and nearly raped and killed by a young man, who I originally thought was a nice guy. I swallowed a spoonful of potatoes and stared at the white table cloth. Things could be worse, but heck, I definitely needed a break.

Even though I didn't have much of an appetite, I managed to clean my plate. Eating kept me busy, so I didn't have too many opportunities to spy on Joshua and Rosetta. When I did pause to glance in their direction, Rosetta appeared to be telling a story she found entertaining. My stomach did a somersault. If the woman only knew what Joshua had been doing the night before—and with whom—she wouldn't have that silly grin plastered on her face.

I sipped my tea. Rosetta would never find out because Joshua would never share the truth, and neither would I. I had decided that last night would be our final time together. There was no reason for me to be petty and vengeful. I really did have feelings for Joshua, and I wanted him and his sweet kids to be happy. If Rosetta could give him that happiness, then so be it.

By the next morning I'd be long gone—and then Joshua and the entire Amish community, would fade into memories.

I quickly wiped the tear from the corner of my eye. It was time to move on.

24

JOSHUA

Sylvia wouldn't let go of my neck. "I missed you, Da," she said in a whiny voice.

"And I you, child. How does your arm feel—and have you been helping your sister with the chores?"

"Oh, yes. I'm doing a lot, mostly things she doesn't want to, like running the hose to the troughs, and I gathered the eggs this morning." She glanced down at her cast. "It's itchy and hot."

I raised a brow at her pouty face. "The doctor told you it would become more uncomfortable in the days to come."

"I want it off now," she demanded.

I disengaged her limbs from around me and lowered her to the floor. "It must heal completely, Sylvia. Be patient and think of other things."

"We have new kittens in the barn," Nora spoke up, and Sylvia's eyes widened.

"Really!?" She ran to the door. "Did mama kitty bring them out for us to look at?"

"Two orange ones and a fluffy gray kitten were playing in the hay just a few minutes ago. I couldn't catch them—yet." Nora grabbed her little sister's good arm. "Walk slowly or you might fall and break your other arm," she ordered.

"No climbing on the bales, Sylvia," I said in my sternest voice. She flashed me a grudging look and I narrowed my eyes. "I mean it."

Sylvia nodded, and I cast a sideways glance at Nora, who winked at me.

They were out the door before I could easily stop them. "Those girls will be the death of me," I muttered.

"Oh, I don't know if it will be *those* girls, but a girl will be your undoing," Nana said. She stood at the kitchen sink, her hands immersed in sudsy water, and her eyes stared out the window.

Goosebumps rose on my arms. I didn't like it when Nana spoke in riddles. It usually meant she was about to chastise someone. I sighed loudly. "What are you saying, Nana?"

She flicked the water from her hands and grasped the towel to dry them before she turned to face me. "I'm an old woman. I've done a lot and seen even more." Her sharp features were stony. "I know people."

I held my breath.

"I've seen how you look at CJ. Her eyes give her away, too."

I remained worriedly silent. All the bravery I'd felt when CJ's warm scent was still all over me had faded a bit. After greeting my children, doubts had crept in. Was I really doing the right thing, or was I being selfish and sinful about a woman who had captured my heart?

When I didn't say anything, Nana looked annoyed, and then she plowed on. "You went to the wedding, and so did CJ." I nodded once, and she looked pleased that I had reacted in a small way. "Did you see each other there?"

"Yes," I answered.

"Did you spend *time* together?" My head snapped up. How could she possibly know? By the smug expression on her wrinkled face, I thought she somehow did.

No point lying, especially to Nana. She wouldn't report me to the bishop—that was for sure. "I did spend time with CJ, and I'm not ashamed to say so."

"Hmm." Her gaze went to a faraway place, and then abruptly returned to me. "You would be ashamed to speak so plainly of it to the ministers...and the bishop."

I shook my head and crossed the room. I stopped in front of the screen door. Nana had a fire roaring in the woodstove, making the kitchen stuffy. Fresh air blew in through the screen, cooling the room. I breathed in the scent of wet grass and dry leaves. My gaze drifted down to the cottage. CJ's car was parked there, but she was nowhere in sight.

My mind cleared. "I'm not so sure. I've been thinking a lot about my future, and what it holds for me and the children." I wiped my sweaty palms on my pants. "I don't know what I should do, Nana."

I looked over my shoulder. When I was a child suffering from cuts and bruises, I'd go to her and she'd make the hurt go away. When I took a wife, and my children came, she was always there to lend a helping hand. And when my wife and baby boy died, she arrived on my porch steps, bags in hand. She moved in, no questions asked, taking up the responsibilities of a mother. Her body was bent with age, and her eyes held the glossy coating of wisdom. I loved my Nana, it was true. I respected her and what she had to say—even if it might not be what I wanted to hear.

Her face softened. "My poor boy. You've had a rough time of it. First your wife takes the life of your boy, and then her own."

I gasped. "How did you know that?"

A sad smile touched her lips. "I already told you. I've seen a lot and I know people." She snorted. "I said nothing of it because what was there to say? Your wife and son were gone, and nothing would bring them back. Forgiveness is the best way. Some things are better tucked away deep in your mind. That was one of those times." Her stare was unflinching. "You handled yourself the best you could, and your children are blessed to have a father who is as doting as you are. But the sins of your wife caused a seed of rebellion to sprout in your own heart. CJ West is a beautiful woman. She's also sweet natured and intelligent. Even for all those things, I don't believe you would have given her the time of day if you hadn't lost your wife and child in such a terrible fashion. I fear you are acting out from raw wounds you still have, and poor CJ will be the one to pay the price for your troubled spirit."

My muscles came alive and I stepped away from the screen door. "I would never hurt CJ." I hesitated. My mouth went dry and my throat became uncomfortably tight. "You're wrong. I have strong feelings for her."

She dipped her head. "Do you love her, Joshua? Will you make her your wife?" When she lifted her head, her eyes were hard and dark. "Because anything less than that will finish that poor girl off. She's experienced more pain and horror in a short amount of time than most people do in their entire life. She deserves better than for you to play with her emotions until you figure out what you want." She huffed. "Men."

I felt like I'd been slapped. To hear my Nana talk in such a forceful manner was disconcerting, but her words rang true. I could have released CJ a while ago, but I hadn't. Instead, I'd kept her close, wanting her to myself, but knowing that I couldn't really have her unless I chose to walk a new path.

I gripped the edge of the table and leaned forward. "I don't know what the right thing to do is. I do love her, but she isn't interested in becoming Amish, and I don't know if I can live in the English world, or if I want my children to be forced to do so."

She walked slowly to my side and squeezed my arm. "It's a difficult choice, and one I cannot make for you. But I will say, love is never wrong. If two people share a pure love and have faith in God, all will work out properly in the end."

A bitter laugh erupted from my lips. "I'm not even sure about CJ's faith. We've never actually talked about it."

Nana smiled, revealing a missing tooth. "There's still time my boy."

"Is there?" I ran my hand through my hair. "CJ might be moving out."

"Then you'll just have to stop her, won't you?"

I shook my head and stared at Nana. "If CJ won't become Amish, then the only other way we can be together is if I go English. Are you all right with that?"

Nana returned to the sink and began working again. "Life with that girl will be an adventure. You'll make memories that you can dream about when you're my age. It's not an ideal situation for you or the children, but neither is being separated from the woman you love. I'm adaptable. That's why I've lived so long." A crooked smile spread on her thin lips. "Can you imagine the headache that will give Aaron? The bishop will not be happy, and that almost makes it worth it."

My Nana's twisted mind and the grudge she held against a man she had a short courtship with seventy years ago made me shake my head. Women could be dangerous creatures.

I grabbed my coat from the peg. "I'm going to talk with her."

"That's my boy."

I paused at the door. "Let's keep this between us for now. I don't want to rile anyone in the community or upset the children. The future isn't set."

"I'll keep your secret." She looked over. "The one you'll have to worry about is Rosetta Bontrager."

25

CJ

I hadn't even made it to my door when a small voice called out behind me. "CJ, do you want to see the kittens?"

It was Sylvia. The girl waved at me with her good hand. Nora was a few steps ahead of her. She gestured for me to follow them into the barn. "Come on!" Nora urged.

I set my duffle bag on the rocking chair and jogged down the steps, heading straight to the barn. The sun was still shining, but it had dipped low on the western sky. Leaves swirled down and the brisk wind carried them away. I picked up my pace and stepped into the shade and still air of the stable. Sylvia peeked out at me from around the corner.

"CJ!" she squealed.

I paused to pat Gypsy's nose and say hello. I would miss the little mare, as well as Joshua's kids. My chest burned and I pushed the thought of goodbyes away. I'd texted Serenity before I'd left Ohio, giving her the heads up that I needed a temporary place to stay in town. Like the true friend she was, she didn't ask questions. She just replied, *okay, I'm on it.*

When I did leave for good, I would probably sneak away like a coward. Goodbyes weren't my thing. Especially for children I cared about.

The sweet smell of hay assaulted my senses when I turned the corner. The stack of square bales stretched into the rafters, and Nora was already climbing up, nearly to the roofline.

"Nora, come down here. You're up too high." I didn't hesitate to scold the girl.

"*Aww*, I'm a good climber," she replied, but she listened to me and changed course downward.

Sylvia tugged on my shirt. "She wasn't supposed to go up there. Da told her not to."

I raised a brow. The girls were always competing with each other for attention.

When Nora was close enough, she said, "They're right up there—" she pointed at a crevice nearly at the very top.

The girls looked at me with pleading eyes. Only for a second, I considered refusing. This might be the last moments I spent with the kids. I unzipped my jacket and handed it to Nora. It was kind of tight through the arms, and not really suitable for scaling forty feet of hay to capture kittens that didn't want to be caught.

"I'll do my best," I assured the girls, lifting my leg and beginning the climb. My ribs still hurt, but the pain was only dull now. Just the same, I moved slowly, avoiding any sudden bending or sharp turning.

I glanced down and saw Nora's smiling face and Sylvia's fearfully puckered one. My luck hadn't been the best lately. I might be pushing it with this catnapping excursion. The hay scratched my arms, and one time I lost my grip and nearly fell. The sound of kittens mewing kept me moving upward, one step at a time.

"Do you see any?" Nora shouted.

"I hear them," I reassured her.

When the kitten noises were close, I peeked into a tunnel in the hay. Shiny eyes stared back at me. From the little bit I could see into the small, dark space, the kittens were just about old enough to be out of their nest, crawling around. I wondered where the mama cat was. At the exact moment I was thinking about her, she suddenly appeared. The tabby trotted effortlessly over the edge of the nearest bale of hay until she reached my hip. She rubbed against me, purring loudly.

"Well, hello there, Mama." I slid my hand down her head and back. Her backside rose high with the motion of my hand. "Do you mind if I borrow one or two of your kittens?" She continued to purr, and I took it as a yes.

I reached into the hole and felt around. When my fingers touched the soft fluff, I grasped a kitten and pulled it out. She was orange and squirming. "I think there's about four in there. I'll bring down two. You can meet them, and then I'll bring them back up to their mama." I held the orange kitten up under my neck while I fetched another one. The second one was solid black and a little calmer than the other one. I murmured to the kittens as I clutched them tightly and began the decent. Mama cat disappeared into her hiding spot.

"What is she doing up there?" an exasperated voice asked the girls.

I didn't need to look down to know who it was. The condescending tone, like I was a child, made my temperature rise.

To my dismay, and from the corner of my eye, I caught the sight of Joshua climbing up after me. *Oh brother. Is he going to rescue me like I'm a damsel in distress?*

"Be careful! You're awfully high up there," he instructed.

I continued my slow journey down. The kittens were settled against my chest and small enough that I could hold them easily with one hand. My ribs began to throb, and I was painfully aware of each movement I made. When my tennis shoe missed the place I needed to step, I fell backwards. With only one free hand, and trying to balance on a wobbly bale with a lone foot, I couldn't catch myself.

I closed my eyes and clutched the kittens harder. Air was all around me, and then strong arms caught me, pulling me close. My eyes popped open and Joshua hugged me firmly. His blue eyes twinkled. "Damn, woman. What were you thinking?" he whispered close to my ear.

There was clapping and squealing below. I glanced down to see the girls embracing.

"You caught her, Da!" Nora shouted.

"You saved CJ and the kittens," Sylvia chimed in.

My heart bounced out of my ribcage when he loosened his hold and carefully lowered me to the ground. The girls rushed forward, and I deposited a kitten into each of their waiting hands. They gushed and cooed at the kittens while I waited for Joshua to step down. When he reached the floor, he stood close to me, too close. I nervously looked between the kids and him, but he didn't move away.

When he continued to eye me, I shrugged. "They wanted to hold the kittens."

He snorted. "You're welcome," he said plainly.

I smiled into my hand.

We sat next to each other on a bale of hay and watched the girls cuddle the kittens. There was a comfortable silence connecting us, and I leaned back and breathed. Oh, how I would miss times like this.

"CJ, you can hold this one," Sylvia said, clamoring alongside me.

I took the feisty orange kitten she offered and made room for her in between her father and me. The small child rested her cast on Joshua's knee and pressed her good arm into my side. "They're beautiful, aren't they?" Sylvia mumbled. Her grasp of the English language was improving, but sometimes her words still sounded forced.

"Prettiest kittens in the world," I said.

"You really think so?" Nora stood in front of us.

"Of course, and I've seen a lot of cats in my life. In Indianapolis, I used to volunteer at a cat rescue."

"Why do cats need rescuing?" Sylvia asked.

"Sometimes people get cute little kittens like this, and then when they grow up, they don't take care of them. Or—" I shot a sideway glance at Joshua "—cats have too many babies and there aren't enough homes for them all." Joshua nodded. "You really should get Mama Cat and these kittens fixed or soon enough you'll have too many to count."

"You're an expert about breeding, huh?" Mirth flashed in his eyes, and he chuckled, quickly adding, "Yes, I'll take your advice and talk to the vet in a couple of weeks."

I was expecting an argument, and was pleasantly surprised by his easy-going manner on the subject. I searched his face and there was something different there. He smiled back at me with a carefree, boyish grin.

The house bell rang twice, indicating that Nana wanted help in the kitchen. The girls jumped up.

"We better go," Nora said.

"I'll put the kittens back," Joshua said. "No worries." He took the black kitten and sat it on his lap.

The girls raced out of the barn, and we were alone.

Before I could say anything, Joshua's mouth closed over mine. His tongue was hungry, and my stomach lurched into my chest. I forgot all about my plans to move out. All I wanted to do was be held in this way, by this man, forever.

His hand caressed my back, pulling me closer. The kittens were trapped snuggly between our bodies. Their purring noises combined with our quick breaths.

I tried to speak, but he hushed me, "Shh..."

Our kiss deepened as his tongue explored every part of my mouth. His sudden aggression was exhilarating and confusing at the same time. The throbbing at my core kept me from listening to my startled mind. I kissed Joshua back like it was our last kiss—and it probably was.

The sound of hooves pounding on the pavement quickly broke us apart. Joshua bent his head, listening. He handed me the black kitten and strode over to the door, opening it wider. Within a minute, his son had reined his horse to a stop and jumped from the saddle.

"John, what's amiss?" Joshua asked.

"It's the bishop." He gasped, working to catch his breath. "His cows got out. They're in the road. Rosetta saw me passing by and asked if I'd retrieve you to help her put them back in the corral."

Joshua looked over his shoulder at me, and I realized it was his way of asking my permission to go. If it had been anyone else needing help, he probably wouldn't have bothered, but it was Rosetta. Of course, Joshua was the first man she'd seek out.

"You should go help her," I said with a level voice.

He tipped his hat and took the reins of John's horse, mounting it smoothly. "Put those kittens back up in the hay. CJ will point out where their nest is," he ordered his son.

And then he was gone in a clamor of hooves.

I handed the kittens off to John and showed him where to go with them. It was an easy climb for a thirteen-year-old boy.

Cool autumn wind greeted me when I stepped out of the barn. I paused, searching the empty road.

Joshua was heading in the direction of his destiny, and there was nothing I could do about it—other than to accept the inevitable and take my own path.

The sooner I did just that, the better.

26

JOSHUA

Rosetta closed and latched the gate after I got the last cow through it. I dismounted and stood beside Desperado, my hand on his sweaty neck.

"That does it."

Rosetta turned and watched me closely. Her cheeks were rosy from the cool air and exertion of shooing the cows. "Thank you for coming so quickly, Joshua. I would have been here all night trying to round them up."

"Where is Aaron?" I asked tentatively. I didn't want to begin a drawn-out conversation. All I had thought about while I worked the cattle was getting back to CJ. I couldn't wait to talk to her, but I was also curious about the bishop's whereabouts. His absence made me wary.

"His brother, another one of my uncles, was in a buggy wreck this afternoon." My brows shot up and she quickly went on to say, "He only broke an arm, but his horse had to put down right there on the roadside. My aunt was at home when it happened. Uncle Aaron decided to take a trip there to help them out for a couple days."

"That's unfortunate, but it sounds like it could have been much worse." I grasped the saddle horn and lifted my foot to the stirrup.

"Wait," Rosetta said.

I faced her, somewhat annoyed at another delay.

She fidgeted with her hands and looked at the ground. "No one's at the house. You're welcome to come in and stay a while." She lifted her gaze. "We can share a slice of pie and a cup of coffee." She took a deep breath. "Or whatever you might fancy."

I pushed dirt around with the toe of my boot. Her invitation wasn't just for a friendly visit. She wanted more than friendship from me—and her uncle being away gave her the perfect opportunity to finally explore her romantic ideas. I briefly wondered what the bishop would say if I took Rosetta up on her offer. The question disappeared from my mind quickly. It didn't really matter.

The sun had set completely and there was only a dull light over the fields. A cow mooed, and then another one. The breeze was sharp, and leaves skipped across the road. I didn't want to play this game with Rosetta any longer. Even if CJ wouldn't have me, I was in no state of mind to begin another relationship.

"I'm sorry. I have to get back to Nana and the children. Being away last night has put me behind on my chores, and the family missed me."

I took up the reins again, not expecting any further conversation, but Rosetta's hand snaked out and grasped my arm.

"Please don't go." Our eyes met, and hers looked desperate. "It's the perfect opportunity for us to get to know each other better." She must have recognized my hard features for another rebuff. Her voice rose and cracked. "I don't want to be alone."

I exhaled slowly and stared at the sky. A sliver of moon and a couple of bright stars appeared. I didn't like hurting Rosetta's feelings, but I had no choice.

"I can't stay—"

She interrupted me. "My uncle will never know, and even if he did somehow find out, it wouldn't matter. I'm a grown woman—a widow. It is appropriate for us to spend some time alone together."

I shook my head. "That's not it, Rosetta. You're a special woman, and I've enjoyed our time talking, but I'm not interested in a courtship. I just don't have those kinds of feelings toward you."

Her eyes rounded and then narrowed. "Is it because you're attracted to your English tenant?"

"That's none of your concern." I swung up in the saddle as my skin warmed with angry heat.

"No, wait!" She grabbed onto my leg. Her eyes were wild. "You'll regret this Joshua Miller. A life with an outsider will bring you down. The attraction you feel for her is from sinful lust, and the desire to have someone who is forbidden to you. The novelty will soon wear off, and then you'll have nothing but a ruined reputation."

I leaned down in the saddle and stared at Rosetta. "Your behavior is unbecoming, your words unfair. I'll follow the way of grace and forget your ramblings. But make no mistake, Rosetta. If you go down the path of gossip and accusations, I'll forever be your enemy."

I spun Desperado around and dug my heels into his sides. He bolted forward into a gallop on the gravely strip along the pavement toward home.

"What of your children, Joshua—have you thought about what will become of them?" She called after me.

Rosetta's words faded as the rush of wind pounded my hot face.

Her last words had struck a chord. Could I really yank John, Nora, and Sylvia from their world of safety and faith because of my love for CJ?

27

CJ

I dropped the pile of folded clothes into the box and scanned the bedroom. It should only take another couple of hours to finish packing. Sure, I wasn't being very neat about it, but I was getting the job done. By morning, I should be on my way.

A wave of depression hit, and I sunk onto the mattress, dropping my head down towards my chest. Everything was supposed to happen for a reason, right? If that was true, I couldn't figure out my purpose for coming here to save my life. Besides a few paintings, what did I even have to show for my time in the little cottage? I had been kidnapped, beaten, and nearly murdered by a psycho serial killer. I'd left Indianapolis to heal a broken heart, and now I had a completely shattered one. The friendships I'd made with Katherine and Nana would soon end, and I would have to let the beautiful children I'd grown to love go, too. It all seemed so pointless and unfair.

I closed my eyes. "I wish I'd never met Joshua Miller," I said out loud.

"No matter what the future holds, I'll never regret our time to together."

I bolted upright, and the blood rushed to my head, causing me to see purple dots where Joshua was standing.

"Go away. You shouldn't be here," I begged.

My vision cleared. Joshua still wore his black coat and cold air clung to him. He hesitated in the doorway and his face was a battlefield of conflict. He regained some composure and took a step into the room. "I can't do that, CJ."

"Why do you keep torturing me like this?" I asked. "We can't be together—so what's there to talk about." My lips trembled and my chest heaved with a deep breath. "Leave me alone," I whispered.

He took another step forward. "There is something we have to talk about. It's important. Please hear me out."

He paused, waiting for my permission. I knew that if I told him to leave at that moment, he would honor my request. He was a gentleman through and through. I opened my mouth, but no words came out. My eyes drifted to the box next to the bed.

He followed my gaze, and then his head snapped back to me. "All I ask is that you hear me out. You owe me that much at least."

"Excuse me?" I scooted to the edge of the bed. "You're the one who pushed me away numerous times because it was a sin for you to be with me—and now you want to talk?"

Joshua held his temper in check, but his jaw twitched. "That's right."

"What about Rosetta—how is she going to feel about us talking?" I felt like I was drowning in jealousy, and I hated the feeling.

"She doesn't matter. I told her just a little while ago that I wasn't interested in a romantic relationship with her."

His words pinged in my head. "How did she take it?"

"Not very well."

A small smile tugged at the edges of my mouth. I hated myself for it, and I wiped the expression away with my hand. "Why would you do that? She seems perfect for you."

"Stop acting like a child." My head shot up and he closed the distance to the bed. He knelt in front of me. He smelled like horses and leather. I tried not to breathe in deeper, fearing my response to his rugged scent and close proximity. "I don't care about Rosetta. I never did." I began to speak and he held up his hand. "You're the woman I love—the only woman I have ever really loved."

The knot that immediately formed in my throat was painful. *Did he just say he loved me?* I could barely breathe and was unable to speak.

"Will you please listen to me?" he asked with pleading eyes.

I sighed and he scooped up my hands. "I've been a fool. I realize it now. I focused on what my community would think and how my actions would affect my children, rather than to listening to my true feelings for you. I don't want to lose you, CJ. I don't—but I still have to be responsible. It's just my way. The differences between us are great. Our experiences growing up and even our beliefs, are not the same. Yet we somehow came together, and I fell in love with you."

He paused, took a breath, and rocked on his heels.

"What do you think we should do?" I whispered.

His gaze fastened on me. "I will forever regret it if we don't try. I wish you would make an effort to live in my world for a little while and see how you like it."

Air rushed into my lungs. I was about to say something, when he cut me off with a more forceful voice. "If you can't handle it or aren't happy, I'll leave the Amish to be with you as an Englisher."

His words replayed in my mind several times. My heart and head debated. There wasn't an easy answer to our dilemma. Joshua said he loved me, and I feared I felt the same way about him, although I hadn't really admitted it to myself up until that point. I closed my eyes and rubbed my temples. We weren't teenagers with a surprise pregnancy—why the great rush?

When I finally opened my eyes, the beating of my heart had

slowed. All along, I had thought that the secret to getting over being dumped by Ryan was by finding another man to take his place. What I had discovered over the past months was that my happiness had to be independent from any relationship I had.

I stared past his shoulders and pushed my curls back. "You know I can't make it as an Amish woman. Maybe if I was younger I could survive the transition, but not at this age. I would be an imposter in your world." His face fell and I softened my tone. "There are things about your way of life I really admire—like the closeness of your people and how they all help each other out. I love farm life and the horses. Your kids are precious, and I really enjoy Nana's company. I have to be honest with myself, Joshua. Even though I have strong feelings for you, I can't live a lie."

Joshua rose to his feet and I suddenly was afraid to lose him. I left the bed and rushed to intercept him. "Can't you just go English first? Why is it so important to you that I practice being Amish?"

His look was pained as he smoothed down his beard with his hand. His answer was reluctant. "There are things about the way I live that would carry through even if I became English."

"Like what?" I persisted.

"I'm not interested in embracing all the modern conveniences you enjoy. I would rather plow the fields with horses than drive a tractor. I want to read at night and not watch the television set." He shook his head forcefully. "Living a life filled with faith and worship is very important to me. If you don't experience my culture, you won't understand the things that really matter to me. You'll just expect me to gladly accept your ideas as best."

"You'd leave your world to be with me if I didn't like being Amish?"

"Yes."

I kind of understood his reasoning, but not completely. "I don't know if I can do it," I admitted.

He leaned forward and cupped my face between his hands. "You don't have to make a decision right this minute."

Joshua's touch made my knees weak. "I don't?" I murmured, looking up.

His gaze drifted back to the boxes. "You shouldn't do anything rash." He bent down and his mouth hovered over mine. "Take some time to think about it."

Our lips brushed and I swayed into him. The kiss was slow and hot. I opened my mouth further, caressing his tongue with my own. He groaned and my fingers went to the buttons on his shirt, when his hand closed over mine and he broke away from our kiss.

I could feel the hard length of him against my hip, and his heart pounded into my palm. His blue eyes darkened to cobalt passion. When he pulled away and left me standing coldly alone, my head jerked sideways.

"We can't keep doing this, CJ." His voice wavered. "I want desperately to make love to you, but that would only muddle our relationship even more than it already is. Each time our bodies join, it makes it more painful to let go."

Tears welled in my eyes. He was absolutely right. The chemistry between us was electric, but that didn't make the decision of what to do any easier.

I nodded and plopped onto the bed, crossing my arms to chase the sudden chill away.

He stood in the doorway for another minute. The room pulsated with raw desire. I knew that I could very easily get him to come back to the bed, but I remained perfectly still, and finally looked away.

"Can we talk tomorrow?" he asked quietly. "Will you still be here?"

I wanted to alleviate his worry, but I couldn't. Because I didn't know where I'd be the next day.

"We'll see…" is all I could muster.

He turned on his heel and left. I heard the door bang shut and I fell backwards onto the bed. This time, when the tears fell, I let them.

The light on the bedside table flickered and then went out. I groaned and rubbed my eyes. The problem with the electricity in the house was annoying, and I couldn't help but think it might be a sign of some kind. Whether fate was showing me how difficult a life without the simple convenience was, or if it was prodding me to consider that I was indeed able to handle the lack thereof, I wasn't sure.

I rolled over and hugged the nearest pillow, being too exhausted to get up and light a candle or even walk down to the basement to check the breaker box.

I'd been crying for an hour. My phone was blown up with text messages from Serenity, wondering what I was up to, but I had ignored them all. My heart was cold and my head too heavy to have a coherent conversation with my friend.

When my eyes fluttered closed, I didn't try to open them. Sleep was the only place I could escape the decision that I had to make.

Would I do anything for love? I wasn't sure, but as the dark fog closed around my mind, the thought of becoming Amish for a short time, in order to have Joshua forever, seemed more and more appealing.

28

JOSHUA

I stared at the ceiling, remembering every look and nuance CJ had had when I'd proposed the idea of her becoming Amish. The way her body responded to mine was proof that she wanted me, but I wasn't convinced that she loved me. Leaving her that night had been extremely difficult. More than anything, I wanted to love her body with my own—but what a mistake that would have been. In a way, it was a bit of a game to win CJ's heart. I hoped she longed for me as much as I did her. The abrupt separation might make her realize how perfectly we fit together, and how she couldn't live without me.

I snorted, doubting that would be her reaction. She was probably fuming angry with me or still packing for her escape. I didn't want to think about the latter of the two possibilities, so I let my mind wander to what Aaron would say if I told him that CJ was joining our community. It wasn't unheard of for outsiders to join the Amish, and the bishop seemed to genuinely like CJ. Of course, he'd be disappointed and maybe even a little offended that I wasn't going to court his niece, but it might not be as much of a surprise to the old man as I worried about. Serenity was another story altogether. I feared her reaction even more because she had enough influence over CJ to change her mind.

My arms ached for CJ, and my skin was tense with desire for her. I rolled the other way and grunted. I should have stayed with her. Even if it was our last time together, it would have been worth it to hold her one more time.

Restlessness made me swing my legs over the side of the bed. I pulled on my britches and crossed the floor to the window.

My eyes adjusted to the darkness outside as I looked down toward the cottage. The lights were off, and the night was quiet. My gaze widened and I pushed the window upwards until I could fit my head and shoulders through. I inhaled deeply, and then coughed.

Smoke. There was smoke on the breeze.

I swung the door open and a cloud struck my face. I coughed and covered my mouth with the handkerchief I pulled from my pocket. The fire wasn't visible, but the smoke was so thick I could barely breathe when I entered the cottage. My legs pounded as I ran to the bedroom. The door was ajar and I wasted no time pushing it open. CJ was still on the bed. My heart jumped into my throat as I made my way to her.

Her skin was cool to my touch as I scooped her up in my arms. I sucked in a small amount of the noxious air and felt dizzy, but I didn't stop moving. Holding my breath, I dashed out of the room, through the family room, and out into the fresh damp night air.

I laid CJ down on the wet grass and gently shook her. "Wake up, CJ. Wake up." Her face was pale and her body limp.

Without training, but feeling the gut instinct to do so, I covered her mouth with mine and blew softly. The action had an immediate effect. She turned her head sideways and coughed. I tugged her into a sitting position just as Nana arrived.

She was wrapped in a night shawl, but her eyes were unusually wide for being awoken in the middle of the night. "I made the phone call. Is she all right?"

I ignored her question. "Stay with her," I ordered.

I bolted upright and ran to the stable. The fire extinguisher was hanging next to the first stall door. I grabbed it and headed in the direction of the cottage's basement door. The amount of time it took to retrieve the extinguisher seemed excruciatingly long, but only a minute had passed by the time I jerked on the slanted doorway, lifting it up. Smoke fanned into my face, and I finally saw the orange flames. Holding my breath, I pulled the extinguisher's pin and dashed into the basement.

29

CJ

My eyes, throat, and nostrils burned. I took the water bottle Nana offered and drank greedily. I poured the rest onto my face. The entire time Nana stood above me, she spoke quiet words of encouragement, and she kept her hand resting on the top of my head.

When I could finally speak, I asked through dry, cracked lips, "Where's Joshua?"

Nana thrust her head in the direction of the cottage. I rose on shaky legs, and she gripped my arm. "No, you mustn't. It's too dangerous."

Tears streaked down my cheeks and I rubbed them with smudged hands. "He needs my help," I whimpered.

"He's an efficient man. He'll be all right," Nana said. Her language changed to German, and without understanding the words, I knew she was praying.

The wail of a distant sirens reached my ears just as John and Nora bumped into me. They were both in their nightclothes. I was relieved that Sylvia wasn't with them.

"What's happening?" Nora asked, rubbing her eyes with her fist. She clutched my side with her other hand.

"Fire in the basement," John breathed. He was about to lunge toward the cottage when Nana stepped in front of him.

"You'll be staying right here, young man. The fire truck is on the way. We can't help your father at this point."

While Nana was preoccupied holding John back, I disengaged from Nora and pushed my legs into a run. I turned the corner of the little white house and aimed for the basement. Smoke swelled from the opening, and Joshua wasn't in sight.

Without any conscious thought, I held my arm over my mouth and stepped into smoky darkness.

"Joshua!" I shouted.

The toxic scent of chemicals sharply burned the insides of my nose. I spotted the billow of powdery spray in the corner, where the breaker box was located, and I caught a glimpse of Joshua's bent form in the fumes.

He stumbled to me. Our arms latched and we struggled together to climb the stairs. When fresh air assailed us, I sucked in hungrily and Joshua coughed violently. His face and arms were bright red.

"Are you burnt?" The words stammered from my mouth.

He shook his head. "It's the extinguisher powder. The breaker box...caught fire, and the pile of logs I had...stored in the basement...went up."

Joshua guided me away from the house and wrapped his arms around me. I leaned into him, wiping my face on his shirt before sneezing.

He laughed. "At least you're all right," he whispered into my ear, lingering with his face in my hair a moment longer than he needed to.

The sound of sirens boomed when the two trucks turned into the driveway. More quickly than I thought possible, men in full fire

protective gear approached us. Joshua told them that the fire was coming from the basement, and that he had controlled it somewhat. The
men pulled hoses across the yard, and began to battle what was left of
the blaze.

An ambulance pulled in, followed by the sheriff's cruiser. I caught
a glimpse of Serenity exiting the car, along with her partner, Todd.
Our eyes met and when her brows arched, I realized I was still in
Joshua's embrace—and then I saw the children.

John and Nora's faces held just as much shock as Serenity's.

So much for keeping our relationship a secret.

I hated being back in a hospital room. The bright lights hurt my eyes
and I was covered with soot, making me feel gross. I didn't complain
about the continued scratchy sensation in my nose and throat, not
wanting to say anything that would make the doctor keep me overnight.

"Can I go home?" I asked.

The doctor looked up from the computer screen. Her facial expression was neutral. "From what the fire chief said, your home won't
be habitable until the electrical system is replaced and the smoke damage is completely cleaned up." She closed the screen and leaned back.
"Do you have a place to go for a couple of weeks?"

"Yes, she does." Serenity walked in and winked at me. "She'll be
staying with me for the time being." She nodded to the doctor, who
she probably knew well, and that was enough for the woman to nod
at me and take her exit from the room.

"I'll have the nurse prepare your discharge papers," the doctor said
right before she disappeared into the hallway.

Serenity stopped in front of me. Her grin was wry. "You really are
either the luckiest or unluckiest person I know."

"It is uncanny how all this awful stuff keeps happening to me," I snorted agreement. "Is it true that the cottage wasn't destroyed?"

"If Joshua hadn't gone down there with the extinguisher, it probably would have spread to the first floor, but his quick actions saved the house—and you too by the sounds of it." She gently shook her head. "But it was also an incredibly stupid thing to do, especially since no one was in the building anymore."

"He's a take-action-sort-of-man," I said simply.

Serenity tilted her head and lowered her voice. "What the hell are you doing, CJ? Everyone saw you two hugging—even his kids."

I slumped on the hospital bed. "I'm sorry. I didn't mean for that to happen, or for the children to see us like that."

"There's no reason to be sorry. I'm not chastising you…exactly." She threw up her hands. "I just don't want to see you get hurt again—and honestly, I don't see this affair ending any other way."

"Joshua wants me to become Amish," I said in a rush of words.

Serenity's mouth dropped open. "That's ridiculous." When I sat still, staring at her, her head rolled back. "You're not seriously contemplating such a thing, are you?"

"Maybe…" When Serenity's eyes bulged and she swung her hands wide, I continued in a calm voice. "He said he wants me to experience his world for a little while. If I don't like it, he promised he'd go English."

Serenity's head rocked. Her rigid expression reminded me of my mother's face, back when I was a teenager and I had some reckless whim that she didn't approve of.

"CJ, I say this as your friend, and as someone who has come to understand the Amish pretty well over the past year. Joshua isn't going to leave his community for you. He might have the best intentions with his little ploy to hook you, but in the end, at his age, he's not going to walk away from his cult-like lifestyle."

Her tone was coaxing and her eyes sympathetic. I hung my head. "That's what I'm afraid of, but…I think I love him," I whispered.

"Love can turn sour very quickly when people start giving up their entire way of life for someone else."

I sniffed in my emotions and hiccupped. Serenity touched my shoulder. She wasn't a touchy-feely type of person, and her little show of affection was taken seriously.

Her hawkish posture softened. "Why don't you think about it for a little while before you do something you'll regret," she urged.

"That's what Joshua said."

"For once he's using his big head, and not his little one." The deep frown she wore proved she wasn't trying to be funny.

I chuckled and was surprised when my ribs didn't hurt. "Is it really okay for me to stay with you for a little while—just until I figure things out?"

"Of course! If you decide that moving away from the Amish settlement is best for you, I know of an apartment in town you can rent." She patted my arm and stepped back. "It's going to fine, CJ. Hang in there. In time, you'll figure it all out."

"Is Joshua still here?"

"Yep. He's in the next room. Daniel said he'd drive him back out to the community."

"I need to talk to him."

"Yeah, I knew you were going to say that." She pointed her finger. "Just don't let him talk you out of taking your time. It's probably the biggest decision you'll ever make."

"I know waiting is the best thing. My head hurts with the craziness of it—but my heart is calmer."

Serenity shook her head as she walked through the door. She glanced over her shoulder. "I really hope in this instance, head will win out over heart."

30

JOSHUA

CJ walked into the hospital room and I straightened my back, resisting the urge to surge forward and wrap my arms around her. "How are you feeling?"

She stopped a few feet away, too far for me to reach out for her. My stomach clenched. Something about her sad eyes and the distance she maintained put me on edge.

"My throat still hurts, but otherwise, I'm fine—I guess."

"You guess?" I said the two words slowly, unsure what she meant.

She shrugged. "I'm glad the cottage was saved. I would have hated to see it burned down. Even with insurance, that would have been terrible."

I continued to stare and wait.

"I've been told I won't be able to live there for a while."

I grunted. "Maybe if I wasn't Amish, that would be true, but I am. I'll have a crowd of men at the farm by tomorrow helping me rebuild the basement, and women to clean the smoke from the upstairs. I'll spare no expense to get an electrician to come out as soon as possible." I pressed my lips together as I tried to lower my voice. "It's my fault.

I should have had someone take a look at that breaker box days ago." My eyes searched CJ's. "You could have died."

She moved a little closer, but not close enough. "Yeah, but I didn't, and neither did you. Serenity thinks it was foolish for you to rush into the burning basement like that."

"The funny thing is, Serenity would have done the same thing. She's always rushing headfirst into danger. I guess she thinks she's the only person allowed to risk her life." I tried to keep the annoyance from my voice, but probably failed. "Did she say anything else important to you?"

CJ exhaled and looked away. My heart thundered in my chest. "She offered to let me stay with her until the cottage is repaired…or until I've figured things out."

"What about us?" I paused, still as a statue.

"I need time, Joshua. We both need time." She took another step. "I can't be rushed—this is important. Can you wait a little while longer?"

I relaxed and my stomach settled. Hope still shined. "I'll wait for you forever."

A small smile crept onto her lips. "It won't take me that long—but I can't make any promises about our future together. You're Amish and I'm not. That's a really big deal."

"It doesn't have to be. You might like being Amish."

She laughed. "And you might like driving a pickup truck."

Now I laughed, and she inched closer.

"John and Nora saw us hugging. I'm not sure about Nana."

I sobered. "Nana already knows about us. I told her the truth. She's a wise old woman and had already guessed what was going on." I stared at the dark sky beyond the only window in the small room. Nana would have the kids tucked back into their beds by now. "I'll talk to them in the morning."

"That's going to be a difficult conversation. It wouldn't be a good idea for the bishop and the entire community to know about us—especially when there really isn't an, *us*, yet."

"I'll tread carefully. My people are good at keeping secrets, even the children."

In a quick action, she leaned in and kissed my cheek. Before she could retreat, I grasped her wrist and pulled her back until our lips touched.

"Don't forget, CJ. I love you."

Our mouths brushed softly, tentatively, and she said, "I think I love you, too."

She pulled from my grip and fled the room. I could still feel the pressure of her lips on mine, and her wildflower scent mixed with smokiness, still clung in the air.

I prayed she'd see the light, and decide to join me in my world. Once she got used to it, and she realized that it was in the children's best interest to remain Amish, she'd fully convert. We would be married and begin our life together.

At least that's what I hoped for, but only time would tell…

Can CJ & Joshua find happiness together in either world? Look for the next chapter of their forbidden romance in 2020.
EVIL IN MY TOWN, the sixth book in Serenity's Plain Secrets is now available, and the upcoming seventh installment in Serenity's story, UNHOLY GROUND, will hit the shelves in 2020.

Thank you for reading!

You can find Karen Ann Hopkins and all her books at https://www. karenannhopkins.com

Made in the USA
Monee, IL
06 March 2020

22806931R00108